VINTAGE
THE WHISPERING CHINAR

Ali Rohila is a Pakistani banker who has previously written *Read No Evil*, a collection of essays published in 2015. He is the descendant of Nawab Hafiz Rehmat Khan Rohila, the Pukhtoon ruler of Rohilkhand. His father, Parto Rohila, was a famous poet and scholar, known for translating into Urdu all the known Persian letters of Mirza Ghalib. *The Whispering Chinar* is his first book of fiction.

T0158492

THE WHISPERING CHINAR

ALI ROHILA

VINTAGE

An imprint of Penguin Random House

VINTAGE

USA | Canada | UK | Ireland | Australia
New Zealand | India | South Africa | China

Vintage is part of the Penguin Random House group of companies
whose addresses can be found at global.penguinrandomhouse.com

Published by Penguin Random House India Pvt. Ltd
4th Floor, Capital Tower 1, MG Road,
Gurugram 122 002, Haryana, India

First published in Vintage by Penguin Random House India 2022

ISBN 9780143452591

Typeset in Sabon by Manipal Technologies Limited, Manipal

www.penguin.co.in

To my father, Parto Rohila, a poet,
a Persian scholar and a littérateur

Kyon Khaliq o Maqhlooq main hail rahein pardey?
Piran e Kaleesa ko Kaleesa se utha do.

(Why should there be any curtains drawn
between the Creator and the created?
Let us remove the priests from their pulpits.)

—Allama Iqbal

Contents

Prologue

The girl crawled across the room as quietly as possible but knocked against a teacup lying on the floor. She surveyed the old man lying on the bed; it didn't seem like he'd heard anything. She slowly opened the door and slided towards the main door in the courtyard. To her horror, the door was locked from the outside. But the height of the wall wasn't enough to deter her objective. Piling up some bricks lying around and balancing a small table on them, she deftly scaled the wall into the narrow street. It was still early, and the streets were almost empty. The fog hung mercilessly, chilling one to the bones. But it was a perfect day for her. She had to make it to the bus stop as fast as her legs could carry her. In her school uniform and white chador, there wasn't much that distinguished her from other schoolgoers.

The bus would take her to the checkpost at the newly constructed dam. From there, she would have to walk till she found some transport to Charbagh. If not, her friend had confided in her, it could take about two hours to trudge down to the village. The physical ordeal didn't trouble her. She just had to be careful that no one recognized her. Just before stepping into the bus, she removed her chador and wore a white burqa that had once belonged to her late mother.

* * *

The guards posted at the checkpost came running towards the car. They bowed and shook the old man's hand, who smiled at them and exchanged pleasantries. He then took out some money from his wallet and distributed it among them. The barrier was promptly lifted, and the car let through.

Armed with poise, the general was amused by the display of reverence playing out in front of him. However, when it was his turn at the checkpost, he was asked to identify himself: the general's civilian outfit could not convince the guards of his bona fide. In his new-found hubris, the general signalled to them to speak with the driver. It was only when he failed to convince them that the seething general had to surrender his self-esteem and show his identity card. He was let through.

1

The Whispering Chinar

The white mansion, reverentially separated from the village by a high wall, stood out in stark contrast to the brown mud houses of Charbagh. Barbed wires, placed on top of the wall, further dissuaded overly enthusiastic intruders. The main gate opened on to a meticulously manicured lawn that was split by a narrow brick path, with rose blooms lining its sides. The lush green turf stretched out solemnly to the stairs of a hospitable veranda that ran along the entire facade. The four imposing pillars that supported the veranda safeguarded the privilege and grandeur of the Khan and his family.

An imposing chinar spread its commanding arms over the lawn. Legend had it that it was planted by a saint known to the grandfather of Khan Sahib, who had told him that the family would prosper as long as the tree lived. Over the years, the glory of the mansion had become entwined with that of the tree, sheltering its inhabitants from the sweltering heat and staying a silent witness to the many stories that unfolded under its span. It was said that the chinar whispered to people who cared to listen. Older family members had firmly believed that its rustling leaves conveyed messages from nature. But the generation that could decipher its whisperings had faded away and the new one attributed the rustling only to the breeze. Thus, when one of the bullets fired by the eldest son of Khan Sahib in order to prompt the maulana to announce Eid al-Fitr had hit one of its branches, it wasn't considered sacrilege.

A large black door in the veranda led to a loft whose height was deliberately set at a level to impress. This large hall was utilized for entertaining men of consequence and served as a rendezvous for the family as well. To reinforce nobility, the walls were decorated with pictures of Khan Sahib's ancestors with their British sahibs.

With the world steadily becoming a busier place, Eid provided the only opportunity for the family to get together. The abundant progeny of Khan Sahib—three sons and six daughters—had grown into an inexhaustible army of grandchildren. The diversity in their individual personalities was united in only one thing: preserving their privilege. And that required, as a matter of right, the presence of at least four maidservants at mealtimes to ensure satiated appetites. But there were other cravings, too, that hadn't ebbed away.

Carrying a genetically embedded desire for land, each of Khan Sahib's sons looked up to his father with expectant eyes. Khan Sahib, over the large span of his life, had inherited as well as accumulated vast landholdings in his personal name. With his health on the wane due to a recent bout of heart issues, his days were likely numbered. It may be added that the division of land, among the sons, was already determined but there were some portions that were still up for grabs. Given his current infirmities, Khan Sahib had handed over the day-to-day running of land affairs to Fahad Khan, which meant equitable distribution of the land produce among the brothers. He took a cut for shouldering this responsibility.

Depending on the weather, the family got together for meals either under the chinar or in the hall. Khan Sahib always sat at the head of the table or, rather, the long line of tables that stretched out in front of him. A large number of charpoys would be arranged on both sides. His children would sit nearer to him, followed by the grandchildren. Seating was always age-related: elders sat close to Khan Sahib.

It was a typical patriarchal set-up. The importance given to men was evident in the seating arrangement as well as the servings of the choicest portions of food. Khan's children had yielded to this well-established order, but his granddaughters would question their mothers about the preference given to their brothers. Such concerns would often be hushed up and the matter chalked up to the universal order of things as desired by Allah.

That year, Eid al-Fitr was celebrated in Khan Sahib's village during the balmy month of September. The announcement was made at the mosque adjacent to the house. The Pukhtoon tradition of announcing a happy occasion, especially Eid, by firing a few rounds of bullets, was the sole privilege of Khan Sahib's eldest son. The sound of the bullets emanating from the mansion was enough for the maulana to announce Eid in tune with the holiday schedule of Khan's grandchildren. The intent justified the action: the children would get another day or two to gorge themselves, as against sleeping on an empty stomach on a dull Ramadan day.

It was Eid, and brunch was being served under the chinar. Having made himself comfortable in his seat, Khan Sahib looked up and surveyed his progeny. From behind those thick-rimmed glasses, the hawklike eyes could discern the seen and the unseen. As he surveyed the hopefuls, waiting for him to take the final bow, his eyes rested on his youngest child, Fahad Khan. This green-eyed boy with blonde hair and a matching moustache was the replica of his mother in form and attribute. Among his children, he strongly believed in Fahad Khan to bear his mantle.

Khan Sahib's own circumstances had been different. Being the only child of his parents and having been bestowed substantive landholdings in a hostile Pukhtoon environment, he had to fend for himself. Over the span of his lengthy career, he had created circumstances that ensured the safety and increase in his landholdings. But now, he had taken a back seat, providing advice to Fahad at his discretion. On his part, Fahad looked forward to completing the last one year of his bachelor's of law (LLB) degree before getting fully involved in the complexities of landed aristocracy.

Khan Sahib smiled wryly as he saw his progeny attack the food. With his own plate full, he assessed each person's personality through their eating habits. They had all filled their plates with greedy exuberance. It had been on one such occasion when he had identified Fahad as the right person for handling and fairly distributing the land produce. They all wanted to be fully satiated with their choice among the served dishes. And as always in a large gathering, the portion of the choicest meat dishes could not match the number. Khan Sahib visualized them as a bunch of hyenas snorting, gnawing and chewing. In the deafening ritual, the four maidservants were constantly kept busy as they ran between the tables and the kitchen, filling dishes, pouring water and bringing warm bread.

* * *

The Eid holidays were numbered. Soon the mansion emptied as the family members returned to their city dwellings. After Khan Sahib's wife's death a couple of years ago, the responsibility of running the affairs of the mansion had fallen on the strong shoulders of Lala. An old, faithful servant, he was considered a part of the family and referred to as Lala, elder brother, by the old and the young alike.

Lala had an emaciated face with skin wound around thinly like wrapping paper. His long nose seemed to be an afterthought, piercing the face and slicing it into two. He had an ugly columella dangling over his philtrum and was in the habit of rubbing his palm upwards against it with a loud snort, persistently trying to rectify the mistake of nature. People who knew him well could tell instantly from this gesture that he was either getting prepared to lie or make a false promise. And he made a lot of promises to everyone. He would always promise to take Khan Sahib's grandchildren on a ride to the lost village of Kiyara, which was now well under water after the construction of the dam, to show them the remains of the great palace that Khan Sahib's family once owned. Now under the ill-conceived dam, the grandeur of the remains was highly exaggerated to keep the children excited about the impending trip, which never came about. The children never asked him how they would be able to see the remains of the palace when it was under water. Fahad Khan would always smile at the oft-repeated story Lala narrated to his young nieces and nephews.

While his two elder brothers had settled in cities, Fahad had decided to embrace the rustic life. He abhorred seeing people come together in confined places for the fulfilment of vague personal ambitions. He called city dwellings mausoleums of the living dead. Fahad cherished the wide-open spaces of the village and loved to take in the fragrances of his orchards. In the absence of his brothers, the attention he received from everyone in the village was addictive. In the *hujras* next to the village houses where the men would gather, village elders, as a matter of respect, would insist that Fahad occupy the charpoy-head instead of the charpoy-feet, despite his reluctant refusals. Elsewhere, he would be asked to mediate between dissenting parties. However, most of his time would be spent standing in for his father at weddings and burials. There would be times when he would have to attend two to three weddings and the same number of burial prayers in a single day. Given the frequency of these rituals and the solemn nature of the people at both, he would sometimes reconfirm from his confidantes if the occasion required congratulations or a prayer. Apart from these social occasions, there wasn't much entertainment for a young man. It was only in winters that Fahad would put together a team of servants and leave for shikar in the surroundings of Charbagh. In the restrictive life of the village, therefore, there was something of interest for him when he spotted Saad Bibi on a swing.

* * *

The chinar not only guarded the mansion but also provided amusement to the household. On one of its branches was a swing that provided hours of pleasure to the Khan's grandchildren during their visits. Surprisingly, the branch supporting the swing had for years weathered the weight of these well-fed children. During the rest of the year, when Khan Sahib was away, the maids enjoyed the hilarity it provided. The merriment surrounding the swing made the chinar quiver with joy, but this went unnoticed. Believing that nobody was watching her at this time of the day, Saad Bibi had removed her veil to enjoy the swing. Within seconds, the tall girl had managed to take it to its full sweep. With her legs firmly perched on the wooden board, the swing was entirely subservient to the command of her lithe body. On every trough, her auburn hair covered her face and flowed away from her as she reached a crest. She sliced the air like a scythe and found pleasure in the oscillation provided by the swing, its movement imitating life in so many ways. Fully immersed in her joy, she was oblivious to the fact that Khan Sahib had entered the house and was slowly walking towards the mansion. Fahad could not forget the horror on her face when she realized his presence. In her amazement, she fell awkwardly from the chinar and swiftly tried to hide behind it, making the episode even more hilarious. Khan Sahib could not help smiling and Fahad laughed out loud from his vantage point in the main hall.

Fahad's first interaction with Saad Bibi took place a couple of days after Eid. One of his nephews, Shuja, had decided to stay back for a few days. At dinner, there were three of them: him, his father and Shuja. Shuja was a few years younger than Fahad and enjoyed being pampered by the villagers. They were seated in the main hall, and Fahad was busy listening to Khan Sahib, as he advised him on some land issues. After dinner, Fahad asked for green tea, which was brought in by the same girl he had earlier seen fall from the swing. Lala had followed her to make sure everything went smoothly. She was modestly dressed and had her chador wrapped around her. With lowered eyes, she presented tea to all of them. When she was serving Shuja, Fahad saw the leer in his look. Fahad was not bereft of these feelings given his own age, but the blatant hormonal nudging of this thirteen-year-old rascal made him wonder what lay ahead. He was sure Lala had seen the look, since he asked him, 'Is your tea not sweet enough?' Shuja's leer transformed into an embarrassed grin. Unaware of the sensitivities of this class, Saad Bibi, while pouring tea into the cup meant for Fahad Khan, clumsily spilled some into the saucer. When she served Fahad, he politely asked her to clean the saucer first. She obediently took both the cup and the saucer and innocently poured it back from the saucer into the cup. As she offered it to Fahad again, everyone burst out laughing. Even Khan Sahib's sombre face relaxed and he smiled. Saad Bibi's jaw dropped, and her large hazel eyes shortly rested on Fahad's face trying to find an answer. Finding none, she quickly left the room. Fahad carried her startled expression in his mind till he went to sleep.

Fahad's room was next to his father's. It was disconnected from the main hall, and one had to walk along a passageway to reach it. The next morning, when he entered the hall to ask for breakfast, he saw Saad Bibi in a combative mode. With her face flushed in anger, her thick eyebrows tightly knitted and the index finger of her right hand raised, she was clearly giving a piece of her mind to Shuja, who, on the other hand, was standing sheepishly, mumbling something.

'Saad Bibi, Shuja! What is going on here?'

'Nothing much, Khan,' Saad Bibi replied, covering her head with the chador that had fallen off her head during the altercation.

'This boy was trying to become a man by targeting me for practice.'

'No, no, uncle,' Shuja whimpered. 'She is like my sister. It is just a misunderstanding.'

'Shuja, before I beat the hell out of you, get out of this place as fast as you can,' snarled Fahad. 'You are going back to Lahore today.'

Shuja darted out as fast as his blubber could take him.

The duty of sending Shuja to the city had to be carried out by none other than Lala, who was asked to escort him to the bus stop. The only saving grace for

Shuja was the protocol accorded to him in the form of his bag being carried by Lala. Fahad saw him depart from his vantage point in the main hall.

* * *

In his youth, Lala always carried a revolver. The leather holster carrying his gun would always be firmly attached to the bandolier that lay across his chest. The tips of the silver bullets shone like armour in the leather contraption, augmenting his formidable presence. He wore a constant smirk, as if only he knew the story of how the world had been brought into existence. To a certain extent he was right. At least he had deciphered what every man had ever wanted. In his youth, all the young girls in service at Khan Sahib's house were personally inspected by him before being given a fitness certificate. His inspection was considered paramount. He loved Khan Sahib and ensured that all the people working at the mansion were worthy of this position. After all, it was Khan who had saved him from his cousins when he had killed two of them in cold blood over a petty land dispute at the tender age of fifteen. He had run away from the land of the slanting mountains to Charbagh, seeking protection. Various *jirgas* were called for his retrieval, but at these meetings, Khan had always politely refused to surrender him. The house was a sanctuary for men and women of the nearby mountain villages: the women running away from abusive husbands and the men from vendettas. Khan had foresight: he could use Lala to his advantage in the future. That he did, and, over the years, Lala became his confidante and consigliere.

Among other qualities, Lala had an exceptional gift for determining the epicentre of tremors arising from lovemaking. He could smell the specific zone of wickedness and easily identify the parties involved. In and around the mansion, there were ample recesses available for wicked intentions to materialize. However, for the inhabitants of the mansion and those associated with it, the vast catalogue of vice remained restricted to fulfilment of carnal pleasures. Lala would initiate his snooping ritual by raising his snout, smelling the air, and rubbing his columella with the palm of his hand before heading in the right direction. He would find the most inconvenient hours of the day to carry out his inspection. His acute sense of hearing and smell led him to the exact spot of the muffled sounds of lovemaking. His duty was to let Khan know about it and then jointly decide the course of action. It was one of these clandestine operations that had led to one of the maids being married off to Khushrang, the imam of Khan Sahib's mosque. Another successful operation had led to a forced betrothal with Khan Sahib's driver; yet another maid was married off to a maulana in a nearby village. And so, the sanctity of Khan Sahib's house had been dutifully preserved. Given the exemplary physical beauty of these mountain dwellers, there was little

Khan Sahib could do to limit the hormonal enthusiasm of his sons.

With a year to go for his LLB, Fahad kept travelling between Peshawar and Charbagh. Every time he was in the village, Saad Bibi would serve him. As expected, they started conversing about small things. It was Saad Bibi who served breakfast to Khan Sahib and Fahad Khan in the main hall. Over the course of their interaction, Fahad found that Saad Bibi had a highly developed intuitive sense.

One day, while serving him breakfast, she asked, 'Why, Khan, you seem to be worried?'

'But I haven't said a word,' said Fahad, surprised by her question.

'You do not have to say something to show you are worried,' she said, her hazel eyes resting on his face for a split second before being quickly drawn away.

'How did you guess?' he asked as he looked up at her in surprise. He was still at an age when surprises came easily. Saad Bibi's ruddy complexion exuding freshness was typical of someone in their early twenties. Fahad noted the placidity of her expression that still managed to convey concern.

'Khan, I might not have read books, but I can read people well.'

Fahad was intrigued by this short conversation; he wanted to know more about her. Until then, he had attributed all forms of intuitive and non-intuitive sense to education only. But now there was something more to be discovered. And so, their conversations started getting longer, making Lala worried. For years he had successfully warded off attacks on the sanctity of Khan Sahib's house against the ever-present threat of a scandal. In this case, although he could certify that Fahad's hormones were in better control as compared to those of his two elder brothers, the fact that he was spending a lot of time with Saad Bibi was worrying him. What perturbed him most was that despite his best efforts during his sniffing ritual, he could not detect any tremors, making the situation even more complicated.

Fahad started visiting the village more frequently. Whenever he would meet Saad Bibi during these short trips, she would reiterate, 'But I am a poor girl, Khan.' Her sad face and downcast eyes would make her seem so innocent. 'And I am not even educated.'

'But you have passed eight classes, haven't you? I will teach you, Saad Bibi. I will teach you English, and we will live here in the village. We do not need to go anywhere.'

'Why do you want to marry me, Khan?'

'Would you stop calling me Khan?' Fahad would say, with mild irritation.

'No, I must,' she would respond with a firm tone. 'You are a Khan, aren't you?'

'Please do not talk about being together,' she would add. 'I will serve you for the rest of my life.'

'But I will make it work.' Fahad's youthful determination would make him promise things he genuinely believed could work. He contemplated discussing the matter with his father and elder brothers. One thing was for sure: he wouldn't back down. He rubbished class differences, believing them to be a facade created to distance people from one another. He strictly believed that all human beings were created equal and should be allowed to live the way they wanted.

'Why do you want to torture me, Khan? I have gone through hard times,' she would say, her agony visible in her wistful eyes. 'I wanted to study but my brother pulled me out from school. He wanted to marry me off to a drug addict for a few thousand rupees. And like so many others before me, I sought the refuge of Khan Sahib's house. They cannot touch me here.' In her anxious moments, Saad Bibi's thick eyebrows would knit together, and she would stare into nothingness.

In Tehsil Swabi of District Marden, only the privileged had telephone connections. Nevertheless, it was an outdated system: all calls had to be made through the operator stationed in the village. The number allocated to Khan Sahib's house was a one-digit number: One. The operator knew everyone in the village and could readily distinguish between voices. His favourite pastime was listening in to calls and picking up juicy gossip. And so, he would frequently listen in on Fahad's calls to Saad Bibi. It was inevitable that he told Lala about it in all its details. 'The plot has reached dangerous proportions,' he would tell Lala. 'The two lovebirds are planning to get married, Lala.

Do you honestly believe it is befitting to the honour of Khan Sahib's house?'

Lala was faced with a difficult situation. He had never faced a circumstance in which a young man had overcome his physical urge to enter a long-term relationship. The absence of furtive sounds and the long telephone calls were making him wary. The situation required much more tact.

A year passed and Fahad completed his LLB degree from Peshawar University. Now he was free to stay in the village. Fahad and Saad Bibi became inseparable. Their amorous escapades could not go unnoticed, and tongues started wagging. But Fahad was an honourable man, who genuinely loved Saad Bibi.

He would hold her close to his bosom and say, 'We will always be together, Saad Bibi.' But she would loosen his grip on her, look into his eyes and say nothing.

'Say something, Saad Bibi.'

'Don't you love me?' he would ask her. But she would just embrace him tightly without saying a word.

Little did Fahad know that he was under a microscope and each of his movements was being registered and documented not only by the chinar but by others as well. One day, Khan Sahib ordered breakfast to be served under the chinar and asked Lala to call Fahad to join him. There was a light breeze, and the whistling leaves of the chinar were desperately trying to convey something.

At his age and position, Khan Sahib was expected to be phlegmatic. His neatly trimmed beard and clean upper lip gave him the reverence required for taking decisions for the village folk. He ensured his head was covered with the customary white cap worn by the Pukhtoons of his district, providing him further credibility in deciding the fate of his people. And Khan Sahib's sharp eyes, behind those thick-rimmed glasses, were known to pierce people with their gaze. Nature had been abundantly bountiful to him. His eyelids doubled over his eye, making them formidable and mysterious. The village folk had a general consensus: they believed he could mesmerize anyone with the intensity of his gaze. In many a local council, his overall appearance combined with his stare and his gruff voice seemed to resolve the most contentious issues.

'But why do you want me to go to Lahore?' Fahad was surprised at his father's insistence. Their shared aim had always been for him to look after the lands. Even now, he was largely running the affairs, taking advice from his father when required. So, he was surprised when his father asked him to go to Lahore to meet an old lawyer friend for career advice.

'You are a capable person, Fahad.' Khan Sahib looked at him admiringly. 'There is no harm in finding out what you can do with that law degree.'

'But I don't want to practise,' Fahad sounded desperate. 'Looking after the land is a full-time job.'

'Take a holiday, Fahad. Go spend some time with your brothers and their children.' Khan Sahib was not leaving any room for negotiation.

Fahad desperately tried to wriggle out, but Khan Sahib's will prevailed.

* * *

The telephone lines were down for many days now. The telephone department was pretty mad with the public works department for cutting the telephone lines—albeit inadvertently—during some construction project in the vicinity. Saad Bibi kept hovering in and around the main hall in anticipation of a telephone call, which never came. She was dusting the main hall when Nasreen, another maid from the slanting mountains, poked her in her ribs. 'You never told us that you were getting married and leaving.' This short, statured girl had been working there for some time. Like Saad Bibi, she also kept to herself and did not bother much with what happened in her surroundings. She was the only one Saad Bibi could speak to with her guard down. Nasreen knew about Saad Bibi's relevance to Fahad but had kept her mouth shut, and that is what Saad Bibi admired. 'Saad Bibi, your brother and your future husband are in the mosque; your nikah is about to be performed.'

* * *

It was unprecedented! How could a woman, albeit a virgin, enter the mosque? The men sitting in a semicircle near the *mehrab* were shocked to see Saad Bibi enter the main hall of the mosque. Her brother tried to get up but was instantly restrained by Lala. Javed, the drug addict, managed some incomprehensible word from behind the drooping moustache covering his ugly mouth. His kohl-lined eyes could still not fully mask the dullness brought about by regular drug use.

'Why did you come to the mosque?' Maulana Khushrang was shocked to see such a beautiful woman enter the mosque. 'This is a clean place, and we do not know what condition you are in.'

'Am I the only unclean one here?'

'Child, you should go back to the house,' said Lala calmly.

'Go back to the house,' growled her brother. It was clear that he could not be restrained for long.

'While my destiny is being decided by you?' cried out Saad Bibi, her frown admirably enhancing her beauty.

'These decisions can only be taken by a guardian, in this case your brother,' Khushrang said, looking at her brother for endorsement.

'Yes, it is so. There is no running away from fate,' her brother added. 'The last time you duped our father and ran away. We cannot let you dishonour us again.'

'So, you are all gathered here to honour me by giving me away to a drug addict? How honourable, brother.'

'Child, we are doing what is best for you,' Lala said, once again trying to defuse the situation.

'Let me decide my destiny. If this is the only choice that you have for me, then I have a better one available.'

And so, with rheumy eyes, Saad Bibi left the mosque to the relief of all the pious men. The sanctimonious religious duty disrupted by a profane girl was carried out without any further disruption.

* * *

Nasreen was the first to see it. It had barely been an hour since she had given Saad Bibi the news. How could it all happen so quickly and without any warning? Running away from marriage and finding protection at Khan Sahib's house did indicate a powerful sentiment but could not be termed fanatical. How could staring out into nothingness be an indication of things to come? How could an absolutely rational person deal with circumstances in such a way?

Perhaps it was her destiny, a sum total of her circumstances. She had desperately tried to break out of it but had failed. Even the rising mist from the spillways of the dam could neither cool down her temperament nor bring about any relief. They say the chinar had shaken violently that day, indicating a prescient warning of some calamity. With a noose around her neck, Saad Bibi's lifeless body was found hanging from the same branch that she had so fondly used as a swing.

2

The Imam

It was customary for Saleem Khan, the eldest son of Khan Sahib, to fire from his Beretta to announce Eid al-Fitr. As per the established norm, he had to wait for Maulana Khushrang to confirm the sighting of the moon before carrying out this action. The maulana was required to cross-examine the people claiming to have seen the moon before giving his approval. But the process was often violated to fit in with Saleem Khan's business engagements. He would ask Lala to arrange for Eid; and the latter would invariably find some stubborn soul in a nearby village who would be adamant that he had sighted the moon. Khushrang would promptly be notified for affixing his religious stamp. Even before Khushrang could reconfirm the veracity of these claims, Saleem Khan's loud notification from the lawn of the mansion would force him to make the Eid announcement.

The village atmosphere would suddenly become festive. Children would go around the village in groups chanting verses from the Quran or religious couplets that were part of the folklore. The day of Eid, following the holy month of Ramadan, was always cheerful. People congratulated themselves on their fasts and the night prayers called Taraweeh. There were instances of minor enmities getting settled on this occasion as well.

* * *

'So Maulana, are you still condemning people to hell, or have you found a better location for them?' Every time Ashfaq Khan met Khushrang, his carefully nurtured wit sprang into action. He was Khan Sahib's brother-in-law, husband to his youngest sister, who had passed away soon after their marriage. With an intellectual bent of mind, his learning years were spent in understanding the inductive and the deductive techniques of philosophy. He had remained fully immersed in the pleasures of the mind, and by the time he had woken up from his reverie, his brothers had usurped all his land. However, Khan Sahib had come to his rescue, and asked him to stay in Charbagh on a permanent basis. Ashfaq Khan had complied but on the condition that he would live at the hujra, not the mansion.

Khushrang was expecting this. Every sentence of Ashfaq Khan that started with 'So Maulana' always carried a blend of sarcasm and humour. But he smiled.

He didn't want to get into an argument because he knew where it would end up.

'So, if you have stopped doing that, which is a sign of doomsday, tell me how is Abdul Aziz doing at the madrasa in Rawalpindi? You should have put him in a school. This village cannot afford another one like you.' The villagers present at the hujra let out a hearty laugh. They always looked forward to this verbal entertainment.

'Ashfaq Khan, the day you start saying your prayers at the mosque, I will pull him out of the madrasa and put him in a school,' answered Khushrang, trying to equal his sarcasm.

'Maulana, I do not intend to alter the universal order of things. Let it continue without any disruption. By the way Maulana, do you know when I stopped coming to the mosque?' Ashfaq Khan's posture changed and his expression became solemn. He bent forward and looked intently at the maulana from above his glasses. As he leaned forward, his hairy ears became even more visible.

'The day Abdul Aziz came to you expecting love, and you showed it in your pious way.'

Khushrang's eyes drifted from Ashfaq Khan's face as he seemed to recall something. His eyes glinted as he placed two fingers on his upper lip.

'Yes, now that you remind me. But he disturbed the Maghrib prayer that I was leading. He spoilt everyone's prayer,' Khushrang said as he ran the fingers of his left hand through his thick beard.

'I am glad you remember.' Ashfaq Khan's intense look remained fixated on the maulana's face, making him uncomfortable. 'The four-year-old was wandering around, looking for his father. He couldn't find you home, so he came to the mosque. He saw you standing in front and a few men standing behind. He didn't know what you all were doing. All he could see was you. So, he ignored all the men and ran to hug you. And you repaid his love by thrashing him. And now you have sent him to that infamous Maulana Abdullah in Rawalpindi.'

Khushrang ignored the previous remark. He didn't feel the need to delve into the past about something that had happened between him and his son.

'Ashfaq Khan, he is a pious man. After all, they are running a madrasa, spreading the word of Allah. Sher Zaman Khan has been very helpful in extending this privilege to us. Had it not been for him, Abdul Aziz would not have been there. That is the best madrasa one can find in this part of the world.' Maulana fidgeted in the charpoy, wanting to end this conversation as soon as possible. He moved his hand from his beard back to his lips.

'Maulana, the way you have dealt with him and the reputation of the madrasa he is in, I foresee an angry young man growing up in an environment that will teach him nothing but hatred and boredom.'

'Boredom?' Khushrang repeated, looking puzzled.

'Yes boredom, the evil of evils. I remember Abdul Aziz always yearned to play cricket with the village boys or video games with Saleem Khan and Sher Zaman's children. But you never let him.'

'That was for his own good. Every father wants the best for his child,' Khushrang murmured with his head bent.

'Wait maulana, why are you leaving so early? Break bread with me today.' Khushrang had sprung to his feet after the comment. Ashfaq Khan smiled and leaned back, resting his arms on the chair. 'The angels won't begrudge you for keeping me company for dinner.' But Khushrang smiled and bent forward to shake hands with him. He could not cope with Ashfaq Khan's sense of humour for long.

* * *

The village folk had always doubted Khushrang's Pukhtoon background. It did not matter if he could speak the language. It was only after Khan Sahib started praying behind him regularly that they reluctantly accepted him as their prayer leader. An imam had to be Muslim, but also a true Pukhtoon to intercede between them and Allah. To put it crudely, it was his dusky appearance that the villagers found un-Pukhtoon. Nevertheless, they did not seem to mind his protruding belly, which was acceptable as part of the persona of the people of his profession. On a practical level, the immense bulge of his belly did limit the vista of his most important part, but without hindering his exuberance for procreation: in seven years of marriage, he had managed to father five children.

Khushrang had been a peasant boy employed by Khan for errands. Given his unlimited capacity to procrastinate, he was often sent to the adjoining village to memorize the Quran. Until that time it was assumed that given the right environment, every child could learn the holy book by heart. In a year's time, the myth was badly shaken. Khan was told that there was no way Khushrang could achieve the objective. So, his stay was extended for another year with the expectation of his brain becoming more receptive through Divine Grace. But when he came back without receiving the anticipated mental illumination, Khan Sahib asked him to become the imam of his newly renovated mosque.

The two-year stay had helped Khushrang achieve a certain level of fluency in reading the Quran. But his knowledge of religion was limited to dubious stories and half-truths about holy men from the earlier centuries of Islam. So, he had to carefully weave the hagiographical content into the fabric of religion to enhance his own credibility among the village folk. The people of Charbagh were too naïve to question the information emanating from the pulpit, especially when Khan and his servants were fully supportive of it. To keep his audience enthralled and entertained, Khushrang had to keep visiting his alma mater to imbibe a regular dose of new stories.

Besides the career, Khushrang's wife, too, had come as a gift from Khan. Rumour had it that Khan's second son Sher Zaman Khan's passion for a maid had resulted in this hastily arranged betrothal. Lala had successfully manoeuvred this move to Khan's satisfaction, saving the sanctity of his house. Khushrang was elevated to the rank of maulana immediately after the ceremony. In seven months' time, the maulana had received a divine gift in the form of Abdul Aziz.

Khushrang's sudden imamate put a lot of pressure on him. To keep his audience spellbound, he had to design sermons full of anecdotes and rhythmic quotes, requiring his thought process to take tangential turns. These sermons would turn into a tirade against the evil of *zindiqs* who, he believed, were slowly taking over the village. By zindiqs he generally referred to the Qadianis, who made up some ten households in Charbagh. On the other hand, conveying the importance of a simple religious practice would take a turn towards vilifying the entire Muslim community for not doing enough. With this objective, he was left with a limited choice of topics within which he could fit in tales, quotes and sketches.

* * *

Khan Sahib had not been feeling well lately. His angina was bothering him, and he was constantly in and out of the hospital in Rawalpindi. When he finally got discharged, the doctor specifically asked him not to stress himself. Both Saleem Khan and Sher Zaman Khan ensured they would stay with him at all times. After all, they were the eldest children and were expected to take care of their ailing father. Back in the village, too, each brother was hell-bent on ensuring that Khan Sahib was well looked after, while also ensuring that the other didn't spend more time with their father. Khan Sahib was not naïve and noticed this pleasant change in their attitude towards him. Although the two brothers continued exchanging pleasantries, the stilted atmosphere didn't allow much conversation between them. And in the condition their father was in, both turned to Ashfaq Khan for advice.

* * *

'So, both of you honestly believe that I am the right person to mediate?' Ashfaq Khan leaned back, intently observing both Saleem Khan and Sher Zaman Khan. The eldest, Saleem, was a replica of his father, while the younger was his distorted version. It is common to find a horrid mutilation of genes in all families. Without anything being medically wrong, genetic receipts assume distortion of features in the coming generation. Sher Zaman Khan was one of those distortions. His balding round head, so typical of his father's, was stuck to a lean body, in stark contrast to his father's broad shoulders. Observing him from behind, the two deep but unnecessary horizontal lines defined the limit of his bald head, while a conspicuous bulge between them identified the demarcation of an almost absent neck. The shape of his eyes was the same as that of his father, but without the double eyelid, making his seem plain and characterless.

Ashfaq Khan continued, 'My nephews, you come for advice to someone who has lost everything to his brothers and lives in Khan's hujra. What words of wisdom do you believe I can give you?'

'But that is precisely the reason we are here for,' said Sher Zaman, shifting in the chair to make himself more comfortable. 'Since you don't have any stake in this, we expect you to be neutral.'

'And you expect me to mediate between greed?'

'It is not greed, uncle. Each one of us should get his right,' said Sher Zaman in a low, piercing tone, his eyes fixed on the ground.

'Both of you have got the best cultivated lands, while Fahad has received ten percent of what he should have received. And of course, your sisters are out of the equation anyway. So, if I take a decision, will both of you accept it in good faith?'

Both the brothers nodded.

'I am sure you won't, because I will try to rectify the injustices of your father, which will not be acceptable to you.' Ashfaq Khan's overbearing conviction did not seem palatable to his nephews, and they felt it was no use arguing with him any further.

* * *

Abdul Aziz lay still in the dark, watching the beam of light flicker on the fan, its rotating blades intent on extinguishing it. The beam would flicker until someone put out the light in the veranda, bringing an end to the amusement. The loud swishing from the fan did little except drown out unwanted sounds. In the sweltering heat, Abdul Aziz wondered about the uselessness of this human invention. The apparatus produced acoustics only, without providing any physical relief. It was as if Maulana Abdullah himself was swishing his cane in the hope of catching someone unaware. The wet towel that he had spread under him was dry now. He slowly raised himself on his elbows and looked around. The other boys were sleeping soundly. How lucky they were to be able to sleep in this heat, he thought. Perhaps they were right. It was not the heat that was keeping him up; he needed to douse his mental flames. In that small room, eight boys of ages ranging from fourteen to sixteen were shacked up together. The proximity of the beds didn't leave any space for privacy, and any movement, especially in the night, was considered scandalous. Conscious of their environment, the boys went to great lengths to protect their innocence. And so, Abdul Aziz silently removed the towel from under him and slowly sank into the hard nylon bands of his bed. The way of the Lord was fraught with difficulties, he was told. It was always the sufferers who found Divine favour.

Maulana Abdullah's vicious caning was legendary. In the initial years of the madrasa, Abdul Aziz had wondered why the soul couldn't just leave the body when the cane was in use and return when it was over. Every caning session was followed by a compulsory session of spiteful humour, degrading the targeted boy to the level of slavery. He distinctly remembered Ashfaq Khan once telling him about yogis who could temporarily die and come back to life at will. He just wished he could do the same to escape the caning.

* * *

The good thing about time is that even the worst gets over. The eight-year-long Dars-i-Nizami course Abdul Aziz was enrolled in at the madrasa was almost over. From a diffident teenager he had now grown into a strong young man. His barrel body amply supported his churlish manner. Given a choice, he might not have wished to borrow the features or colour of his father, but since he was living God's will, these satanic matters had to be tossed aside. His vociferous and vitriolic nature had helped him extract benefits even from the madrasa: he was now the lone occupant of a room which was as big as the one eight of them had slept in. He didn't need to look up to the fan for amusement any more, and it didn't matter how many times he twisted and turned in his bed. No one had the audacity to question Abdul Aziz.

As Abdul Aziz reminisced about the past, he tried to come to terms with his father's methodology of converting him into a perfect Muslim. In those early years of his life, Abdul Aziz had fancied finding a way to break out from the miseries of day and night. Winters were especially harsh. Every morning before dawn, he had to reluctantly leave his warm bed on a signal from his father: a direct hit with his slipper. He vividly remembered quivering through the azan and being unable to pronounce the words as his teeth chattered. He knew Khan's grandchildren wore shiny coats that kept them warm. They called them jackets but one couldn't find them in the village. Once, when he had got up late for calling the azan for Fajr prayers, his father had whipped him to his heart's content, blaming him for staying up late to play video games with Khan Sahib's grandsons. He was still too young to ask him if God had specifically notified him to wake up his son for the sacred ritual or had stopped him from carrying it out himself. There were other correctional rituals as well, but this one was particularly harsh. For days his back had ached, and he couldn't even lift his arms to his ears while calling the azan. He wondered if that was God's way of punishing him for his slackness.

He recalled the boredom his father's Friday sermons brought upon him. Unable to stop his father's sermon he could only yawn and soon, to Khushrang's frustration, the entire mosque would be yawning away his religious symphony. As if on cue, his audience opened their mouths unabashedly as soon as he turned his head in their direction. To an outsider it seemed like a silent opera where each group of people would open their mouths right when the conductor looked in their direction. The receptive audience seemed to be hooked to Khushrang's head movement, fully appreciating the concert. Fortunately for Abdul Aziz, his father could never locate the source of this contagion.

As a young boy, Abdul Aziz always looked forward to the visit of Khan Sahib's grandchildren. He would be fascinated by the toys they had, as he had never seen anything like them before. The cycle tyre and the stick that he used to steer it with seemed so absurd compared to these gizmos. The Khan boys seldom included him in their activities, but he would just sit there and watch them play. He would wait for that moment when one of them would ask him to join them. How he yearned to play with their toys.

Abdul Aziz spoke chaste Pushto, which these city dwellers found amusing. His presence became relevant only when the boys wanted to have fun by learning vulgar street words. Otherwise, his role was limited to fetching water for them from the kitchen and carrying their toys from one place to the other. At mealtimes, the boys would savour the dishes made especially for them, while he would be asked to come later. With his head bent downwards, Abdul Aziz would quietly walk away.

As they grew, these children started talking about careers and universities whose degrees suitably equipped one for a better future. Hearing them, Abdul Aziz strongly felt that he, too, was being equipped for the future, but with a difference: while they were being geared up for the temporal, he was being prepared for the eternal. Humans were meant to spread the word of Allah and in doing so, He would shroud them into His Grace, solving all the earthly issues; Abdul Aziz's own father being a case in point. Abdul Aziz's inchoate awareness of religion brought upon him mockery initially. The Khan boys would often make fun of what he had learnt at the madrasa. His argument would be rubbished, making him feel as if he were from another world, speaking some other language. And then, one day, he decided that he had had enough of the Khan boys' ribaldry and derision. He promised himself never to visit the Khan mansion again.

But that again was a long time ago, and the past seemed like a different world altogether. Now he had learnt to hide his fascination. The Khan boys seldom visited the village, and when they did, they hardly met Abdul Aziz. Even when they did, Abdul Aziz remained formal. If they tried to invoke the past, he smiled it away, without delving into it.

In his last couple of years at the madrasa, Abdul Aziz had found a new level of self-confidence. Everyone around him could sense his ferocity, amply supported by his physical strength. His peers and teachers held him in high regard. Stories about his notoriety had even reached the village. He had become Maulana Abdullah's confidante, carrying his personal messages to other imams in Rawalpindi, and in other cities as well. During the compilation of the list of troublemakers by the police, his name was closely identified with Abdullah's, which he was always very proud to mention. And it was during this time that his heart opened up to the pleasures of the temporal world. For once, he realized the potential of religion in leading a comfortable life. After all, every prayer compulsorily included asking Allah for the best in this world and the eternal one, in the same sequence. If one couldn't make living here worth its while, one would be a failure in eternity as well.

* * *

Sher Zaman had helped Khushrang send Abdul Aziz to the madrasa and in paying for his expenses during his entire stay. It wasn't much, but Khushrang could not even afford that paltry amount. Despite that, Abdul Aziz hardly ever paid Sher Zaman a visit. He found it difficult to forget the leer in his eyes when, as a young boy, his mother had taken him to visit the ailing wife of Khan Sahib. At the time he didn't understand the meaning of those looks. He only remembered his mother's tight grip around his hand, quickening her pace to leave the mansion as fast as her feet could move.

Although Abdul Aziz had vowed never to return to the mansion, he felt pressured when Sher Zaman sent someone asking him to come over. With a heavy heart he paid him a visit.

* * *

Khan Sahib's mosque was one of those spaces in the village life that brought about temporary harmony across varied temperaments. Khushrang had been looking after the affairs of the mosque for several years now. The simple villagers reciprocated to the passion of the pulpit. They looked up to the pulpit for giving them hope in this world and the hereafter, which they did receive in a language they could understand. But there was a commotion after the arrival of Abdul Aziz. Khushrang, who had not been keeping well for some time, was relieved to ask his son to lead the prayers while he recovered. Finding his opportunity, Abdul Aziz slapped the simple folk with the knowledge he had gained at the madrasa. He found fault with almost everything the congregation did and admonished them for their lack of understanding of religion. No one was spared. An old man was seen crying and murmuring to himself, 'I have been carrying out the ablution rituals incorrectly, and my prayers will not be accepted.' The poor man couldn't believe it when Abdul Aziz handed down the verbal fatwa to him. On the other hand, the more stubborn were heard saying, 'We knew it all along that one can either be a good Muslim or a good Pukhtoon; both cannot go hand in hand.'

* * *

The nation's procreational enthusiasm did not leave Charbagh behind. The village had expanded over the years and the numbers had increased considerably, making it increasingly difficult to house all of them at once in the mosque, especially during Juma prayers. Either the mosque had to be expanded or faith had to be mellowed down to cope with the rising number of people in the mosque. With some now working in the Middle East, the villagers were also getting a taste of new-found wealth. Sher Zaman saw this as an opportunity. Instead of bickering over judicious allocation of land with his elder brother and an ailing father, he saw leverage in utilizing religion judiciously; and what was better than bringing Abdul Aziz closer to him.

'I see that a mosque is now being constructed adjoining your newly built villa.' Ashfaq Khan looked with amusement at Sher Zaman. Before he could respond, Ashfaq Khan came up with another one, 'So, you want your house to be on your own land and the mosque on disputed land? That is clever.'

'We need another mosque in this village. This one is becoming too crammed for comfort. People have to stand outside now.' Sher Zaman was quick to provide his justification.

'But on disputed land? Something you and Saleem have been arguing about and discussing with your father as well. It doesn't augur well for the family and for the village.'

'It will be for the good of the people. Plus, God will reward me with a house in paradise.'

'It is fascinating to see your greed transcend your earthly career. You are prompting the angels to reassess your deeds after you have entered paradise with dubious credentials.' Ashfaq Khan's jest didn't sit very well with Sher Zaman. Ignoring the remark he said, 'Uncle, everything shall remain the same: father will serve as imam in one mosque, son in the other.'

'No nephew, it won't,' Ashfaq Khan whispered, leaning forward to make a point. 'The village will have two religions when your mosque becomes operational.'

* * *

In the backdrop of this conversation, Sher Zaman's offer to Abdul Aziz was too good to be true. The mosque was new and much bigger than Khan Sahib's. Sher Zaman offered Abdul Aziz a handsome amount every month and a year's supply of grain. The living quarters were much better than what his father had been given by Khan Sahib. For a recent madrasa graduate, a new mosque and living quarters were the best employment opportunity life could offer. Abdul Aziz pondered how many of his classmates could get this break in life? Most of them would get associated with some fastidious imam in their home towns, spending all their lives hoping to become one. Some would not even find that position, moving from towns to villages to hamlets in search of a mosque. Only the more enterprising ones would find some unclaimed piece of land in a city and build a temporary structure for a mosque. In due course, people in the locality would pitch in money to build a permanent structure and institute a permanent pay structure for the imam as well. Even a flimsily built temporary structure with corrugated metal sheets utilized as a mosque could not be reclaimed by any authority.

It wasn't long before Ashfaq Khan's prescient statement came true. Father and son were now managing the two mosques, but their outlook was different. Soon after Abdul Aziz took over Sher Zaman Khan's mosque, Eid al-Fitr was to be announced. Saleem Khan had fired the shots from his pistol, prompting an ailing Khushrang to announce Eid. The same evening, Abdul Aziz, wearing a black Arabic robe, proceeded to announce the unavailability of any credible evidence of the moon being sighted. Khushrang sent a messenger asking Abdul Aziz to announce Eid as well, which was politely refused. Abdul Aziz later made the announcement without consulting Sher Zaman. It was mere coincidence that it suited Sher Zaman's circumstances.

The morning after, Saleem came to the mosque accompanied by Lala. Khan Sahib was too weak to walk up to the mosque. With a place reserved for him in the first row, Saleem was surprised to see the number of people in the mosque. He knew that Abdul Aziz had made an announcement on Sher Zaman's orders but could not believe that the once swarming mosque was only half full. The privilege of Khan Sahib's house stood irrefutably damaged.

3

The Tears of Nazo

Nazo lay on the floor while the cards were being dealt. She waited a while before picking them up and cautiously turning them over. On her turn, she closed her left eye and held her tongue between her teeth. The other players, anticipating a spectacular hand, heaved with relief as soon as she showed her hand. It was a modest one, and she let out a hearty laugh. She tossed her long, thick hair from the left shoulder to the right and back again, as she shifted her weight on her elbows to make herself more comfortable. Her roving green eyes were constantly reading the expressions of her fellow players. Many a time her eyes would meet Shuja's, and she would coyly drop her gaze back to her cards. Shuja was constantly cracking jokes, and everyone seemed to enjoy them. The cousins had got together on Eid after a lapse of a few years and to their own surprise everyone had grown up. The chubby Shuja, Sher Zaman Khan's son, had grown up into a handsome young man, and so had Nazo, Saleem Khan's daughter. From a cowering little girl, she had transformed into a confident young woman. Although Shuja and Nazo had met each other more frequently than the rest over the years, on this occasion, he just couldn't take his eyes off her; the constant flow of jokes was meant to keep her attention riveted to him.

Times had changed: a generation before, these boys and girls could not have imagined mixing freely in an unchaperoned environment. In a joint family, cousins would pretend to be brothers and sisters till the time some would get betrothed to each other. The elders, who took these decisions, would invariably assign them to the will of Allah. It was never explained how they managed to read His will. Such sibling to spouse arrangements almost always created problems for both partners, who found it exceedingly hard to come to terms with the appropriate response expected of them. This was the situation Saleem had found himself in when he had got married to his aunt's daughter, Naheed. By getting his niece to marry his son, Khan Sahib had managed to keep a large tract of land within the family. The widowed sister living with Khan Sahib had considered the arrangement to be a privilege bestowed upon her daughter. Naheed had thrown tantrums at the time, but her opposition was cleverly set aside. It was said that she had wanted to study at the National College of Arts at Lahore, the premier art education institution in the country. She was known to sit up all night reading about art or working on her paintings. Nevertheless, by the time she realized her dream, the patriarchal set-up had usurped another victim.

The new generation was the product of English-medium schools. Their contact with their language and culture was limited to spending a few days in the village. Even then, some of Khan's children had strictly forbidden the use of any other language except English in their homes. Hearing their children speak fluent English made them proud. It made them even more proud when they heard them make fun of people mispronouncing English words.

These children were hooked to English movies and books, transforming their fantasies around everything the West had to offer. So, despite having an army of servants running around, catering to their every need, they still dreamt of absolute freedom. They had no interest in discovering the local areas like the mythical valley of love, Karamar. Instead, they preferred being teleported as protagonists of the stories of *Cinderella* and *Rapunzel*. To them, the valour of the indigenous warrior seemed hollow as compared to the exploits of Superman; their sprawling village mansion worthless when compared to a small apartment in New York; and their lifestyles as drab as it could get. Caught up in this dilemma, their parents tried to strike a balance between the old and the new by sending their sons to mixed gender English-medium institutes and their daughters to the all-girls' Jesus and Mary schools. They sincerely believed this step vital, not only for preserving the traditional set-up but also for accommodating the new generation's modern aspirations. Girls of Charbagh were encouraged to imbibe the best available English language skills but only under the watchful eyes of Christian missionaries. Although they were free to practise their faith, introduction to Western thought still made them conscious of a woman's need for emancipation. Little did they know that later in life their mindset would be considered elitist and that this closely knit sorority would ultimately alter the carefully nurtured morals of the society.

While the group was playing cards, Saleem's wife and Nazo's mother, Naheed, entered the room. The moment she came in, Nazo sat up straight and covered her head with a dupatta. The lively atmosphere in the room suddenly became sullen. The boys put down their cards and quietly left the room. No words were exchanged, but the message of strict segregation was conveyed effectively. After a while, the girls too left. Left alone, Naheed looked up and her eyes rested on the rustic scenery on the wall. The almost perfect village scene was smudged in two places. On closer scrutiny, one could discern that the smudges were an afterthought. As she slowly moved close, her eyes noticed the bold N at the bottom of the picture. Adjusting her hijab, Naheed gently touched the smudges and took a deep breath. She pursed her lips and lifted her neck—the physical resolve indicated the smudges to be atonement of a sort. She murmured to herself, 'Alhumdolillah, I have implemented God's will by removing the figures from my painting.'

As always, it was a short interaction between the cousins. The world was moving at a fast pace, squeezing out leisure from the lives of its inhabitants. Nazo's college was to reopen shortly after Eid. After completing her A levels from Jesus and Mary, Nazo had joined a business college in the university at Islamabad. Unlike her younger sister, Afshan, whom Saleem preferred to keep at home, Nazo had spent all her life in a hostel. First it was the school at Murree and now the business college in Islamabad. She spent most of her summer holidays in the village, while her other siblings remained home. She could never understand why in the presence of so many grandchildren, her father always forced her to take care of her grandfather. It was as if she was being deliberately kept away from home.

* * *

Shuja, the eldest son of Sher Zaman, was Fahad Khan's favourite nephew. He liked spending time with him in the village. It was here that Nazo and Shuja developed a deep friendship and started calling each other buddies. In the absence of an appropriate noun indicating a relationship between a man and a woman outside consanguineous ones, either in their mother tongue or the national language, they didn't have a choice but to borrow it from elsewhere.

The only way of communicating in those days was through letters or phone calls. Shuja, being a day scholar at a medical college in Lahore, had the luxury of calling Nazo at her college. But he was constrained by the number of times Nazo could attend to these calls at the warden's room. The sly warden preferred staying in the room every time Nazo answered a call, limiting their conversations. He always introduced himself as her brother. The warden, an elderly lady, was deeply suspicious of these calls. After all, how could a brother and sister be so happy and giggly talking to each other. And if she was not mistaken, sometimes the sister would not even ask about the well-being of her parents.

What Nazo liked the most about Shuja was his pithy one-liners that almost always tickled her funny bone. He had the talent to find a humorous angle to any situation. He was mesmerized by her green eyes and her fluency in English. For the new generation, English was the language that offered possibilities of pleasure. The copious volumes on love in the local languages did not have the vocabulary of love intertwined with pleasure. They only defined the parameters of forbidden love. Love was duly admired in folklore, but only when it ended up in physical and emotional suffering. The lovers were expected to suffer instead of having a satiated physical relationship, albeit a legitimate one. Society considered puritanical love to be beyond the physical realm. Such norms created a need for new vocabulary to gratify the needs of modern minds. And it was only through the medium of English that adolescents could make more meaningful demands of each other.

Nazo was well read and eloquent as well. For Shuja, she was the protagonist of an English movie: bold, beautiful and independent. He found her to be more liberated than the girls he had come across. She was mentally emancipated and perspicacious: her business studies did not limit her insight into literature and history. Ultimately, it was the English language that brought them together. Shuja himself was fond of novels. It was as if two foreigners in a faraway land, from a common background, had discovered one another. Their appreciation for each other's fluency of the language through common love for novels brought them closer.

The next year, Shuja and Nazo kept meeting on occasions in the village. With studies taking up most of their time, it was not possible to spend much time in the village. And with so many cousins around, it was difficult to have any meaningful conversation anyway. They tried their best not to invite attention from anyone. But these matters are not possible to hide.

Naheed had seen it and ignored it. Farhana, Sher Zaman's wife and Shuja's mother, saw it but couldn't keep it to herself.

'Naheed, I am getting very uncomfortable with the situation.' Farhana was visibly upset.

'Aren't you reading too much into it?' Naheed was evasive.

'Can't you see it? It is so abundantly clear.'

'They are still young.' Once again, Naheed tried to limit the conversation.

'That is exactly what I am worried about. Hope they don't take any stupid decisions or actions.' Farhana was determined to conclude the matter.

Delicately cast into the human form, Farhana was the typical memsahib. She was an alumnus of a convent school in Lahore and had graduated from Kinnaird College. Her father was a district management group officer and at one time had served as assistant commissioner in District Mardan. It was here that Khan Sahib had managed to forge a good relationship with him, which had ended with marrying Sher Zaman to his daughter. The relationship had helped Sher Zaman interact with the crème de la crème of Lahore society. It was Farhana who had taught Sher Zaman all the social graces. At times, she would laughingly mention how she had spent her entire life rounding off the rough edges of the men of Charbagh.

On a typical social evening, Farhana was known to tie her hair in a bun. The expensive saris she wore required the neck to be bare, to show off her blouse. She would be heavily decked up for such occasions and add a cigarette to further establish her presence.

However, when visiting the village, she had to remain simple, which she did with reluctance. But this self-love did not diminish her protective tendency. She had to see her children better off than her, both in terms of education and their social set-up.

Naheed's disinterest infuriated Farhana and she left the room. She then spoke with her husband about it but even he did not seem to take the threat seriously.

'She is Saleem Khan's daughter. What is the harm?' His nonchalance infuriated her even more.

'Saleem Khan's daughter! Really! Is that the only merit left in the world now?'

Farhana gave an incredulous look. They didn't have any further discussion on the matter.

* * *

Meanwhile, Shuja had entered his third year of medical college, while Nazo had taken admission for a degree in business administration. Given Shuja's good performance in his second year—considered to be a nightmare for medical students of the time—Saleem had bought him a Suzuki FX. Lately introduced into the local market, the car was the newest product aimed at squeezing human ambition. The world was gripped with miniaturization. Along with these cars, apartment buildings were introduced into the Pakistani market, outside the port city of Karachi, for the first time. The lofty ambitions of a generation were now being cut to size. Nevertheless, for Shuja, the gift could not have come at a better time.

* * *

'So, you came to Islamabad to see me.' Nazo smiled and glanced sidewards as she leaned on to the railing, her hair fluttering in the light breeze of a sunny winter afternoon. Daman-e-Koh was quiet as expected. There was one other couple who had preferred to stay in the car, far from the prying eyes of strangers. This place established by the city council provided a view of the entire city. On a clear day, one could see some settlements of the city of Rawalpindi as well.

'Not really. I came to count the baboons in Islamabad.'

'There are no baboons in Islamabad, only monkeys.'

'I want to document their genetic transformation from baboons to monkeys.'

Such was the conversation between two youngsters whose sole aim at the nascent stage of the relationship was to keep the other interested in them, forever. There was no timeline defined for *forever*.

Shuja started visiting Islamabad more frequently. He would stay at Rawalpindi Club and drive to Islamabad to meet Nazo. Time passed and now both were in their final year, expecting to graduate soon.

Shuja had tried speaking to his mother, but to his surprise she had outright rejected his proposal. In fact, she had vociferously denounced Nazo to the extent of telling him not to mention her name again in the house. He could not understand her reaction. If such arrangements had worked for the earlier generations, why couldn't they work now?

He always knew the whole family was beset with complicated relationships. The seemingly affectionate scenes of sibling love were played out well by the elders of the family. But once they left the village, this love would turn into contempt. The children were quick to pick up these family issues, defining and adjusting their own role in it. The two elder brothers and their six sisters were constantly aligning and realigning their interests with each other to gain maximum advantage when the distribution of land would eventually take place. The sisters especially were wary of the elder brothers. And to rein in support from the right sister at the right time in the future, the two brothers would send them gifts on certain occasions. It was not only the sisters who had issues with the brothers; even the two brothers had issues with each other. To make up for their perceived loss, each would clandestinely vie with the other to find those precious moments with their father, providing them the opportunity to get his signature on stamp papers for a portion of some prized property. There were instances of revocation of some earlier inheritance as well. These clandestine operations were being carried out by the two brothers much before the major chunk of land and property was to be distributed at the time of inheritance. Both took advantage of their father's ill health to the maximum, thereby complicating family relationships.

Given this background, Shuja and Nazo were unsure of the family reaction if they decided to make their desire for each other public. Shuja was still shocked by the reaction of his mother and wasn't sure how to deal with it.

* * *

The maulana of Jamia Masjid had two basic questions: Who was the girl's *wali* who would give her away, and who were the witnesses? Shuja and Nazo were both trumped. They abandoned the plans for a religious ceremony and decided to go for a civil marriage. The plan was to keep everything under wraps till such time when both were independent enough to shoulder responsibilities. But news travelled fast. Someone from the family snitched on them. A family council was summoned and both Shuja and Nazo were asked to appear in the main hall of the village mansion.

* * *

It was a family council in name only. The meeting was attended by Saleem, his wife Naheed, Sher Zaman, his wife Farhana, and the newly married couple. The meeting went worse than expected. Everyone was speaking at the same time, and nobody made sense. On two occasions, Farhana just couldn't restrain herself and slapped Nazo, before being held back by her husband. It was one of those rare occasions when Farhana let go of her poise. Naheed couldn't be left behind. Even she had her fill hitting the poor girl before being pulled away. Shuja, who was expected to defend Nazo, stood by with his head down without even a whimper.

It was only after the physical altercation had been brought to a halt and the shouting match had subsided to a degree that the demand from Farhana became clear. She turned towards Saleem and asked him pointedly, 'Saleem lala, all we need is a simple answer. Is Nazo your daughter or not?' Her flushed face was brimming with anger and her flared nostrils had become even more conspicuous.

With a shocked look, Nazo looked at Farhana and then at Saleem. She couldn't believe her ears. With tears streaming down her face, she tried to wipe her eyes with her dupatta to have a better look at the scene being played out. No one in the room was willing to pass a tissue to her. To have her paternity questioned after having spent twenty-two years of her life with Saleem and Naheed as her parents was outrageous. The council was, as she had believed till then, supposed to reluctantly confirm their marriage. She had expected a mild altercation at the most. Before coming to the meeting, Shuja and Nazo had thoroughly rehearsed the anticipated inquisition. But this was a bolt from the blue.

Saleem just lowered his eyes and didn't say a word.

'Saleem lala, please tell us if she is your daughter or not?'

Once again, Saleem kept quiet.

But Farhana's frontal lunge at Saleem had brought up an issue thought to have been settled a long time ago.

Naheed looked up at Saleem.

'Now you have to settle this. I always told you not to bring up this snake in our house. But you always insisted.'

'That is why I tried to keep her away from the house,' he mumbled.

'But it was not enough to settle the issue. This is what impurity of blood does to a family.'

Amidst sobs, Nazo pleaded, 'Baba, what is this? Why is Farhana aunty questioning my paternity?'

'You have committed *zina*,' Naheed seethed with anger.

'We are married. Shuja, please show them the marriage certificate.'

'You can make these certificates for a mere hundred rupees. In the absence of a nikah, it was nothing but adultery. You deceived my poor nephew. You bewitched him.'

'You are my mother; how can you say that?'

'I am not your mother. You should never have lived with us.'

Sher Zaman interjected, 'Saleem lala, we have had enough of this melodrama. Please get it over with.'

Nazo couldn't understand what was going on. She had been brought up in Saleem's house as his daughter. As far as she remembered, she had always called him Baba and Naheed, Mama. In a flash her whole life played out in front of her, and she realized how stupid she had been not to understand how her own family had consistently disowned her. First, she was sent to a hostel at a very young age. She remembered crying for hours in her hostel bed. It was one of the sisters, a comparatively younger nun, who for years had provided that much-needed physical touch to calm her down. She distinctly remembered the soothing voice of the nun who read her Christian prayers to make her go to sleep. It was in Latin, and she could not understand the words. But the tone and the rhythm remained in her mind for years to come. This was in stark contrast to the Ayat ul Kursi her siblings would recite, without understanding its meaning either, before going to sleep.

Her male siblings, Farid and Humayun, maintained a cordial relationship with her, but her mother and sister, Afshan, were always mean to her. Sometimes they would make it so obvious that she would feel like an outsider. But it was Saleem who would treat her well and make her forget the unfairness.

This was a moment of epiphany. She realized she was a stranger in the realm of the Khans. Before Saleem could answer, she got up and pulled at her father's sleeve. 'Baba, Baba,' she cried.

'Baba, Baba. I don't understand. What are they saying . . .?'

'Am I not your . . .?' Amidst a constant flow of tears and a choking throat, she could not complete the sentence.

With three of the four family members looking askance, Saleem was left with no choice but to respond. He tapped Nazo's head lightly, moved towards Shuja, put his hand on his head and said, 'With Allah as my witness, let me make it clear to you all. Nazo is not my daughter.'

Nazo leapt at Saleem and hugged him, crying uncontrollably.

'Baba, don't say that. Please don't. Please tell them that I am your daughter.'

The situation prompted Farhana to swiftly get hold of Shuja's hand, press it hard and tell him hoarsely, 'You have to divorce her right now.'

Nazo could only manage to say, 'Chachi, please don't do it. Shuja, please don't. Baba, please tell them you love me.'

'Stop calling me Chachi.'

Saleem just stood there, neither putting his arms around Nazo nor pushing her away. His shirt was wet from her tears. She wouldn't let go.

Nazo had expected some support from Shuja, which to her surprise wasn't available during this entire episode. With his head bent, he just sat there, breathing. She tried to remind him of his vows of support for her, but he kept quiet. He had found the reaction to his marriage so overwhelming that his love for Nazo had got buried forever. Deeply under the influence of his mother, Shuja repeated the religious mantra three times to throw Nazo out of his life forever. The sanctimonious word, talaq, repeated three times to end a relationship came in handy for the occasion, making it convenient for Farhana to reclaim the family honour.

They say walls have ears. Ashfaq Khan was promptly told about the episode. Without wasting any time, he raced down to the mansion. Boldly entering the room, he picked up a sobbing Nazo, grabbed her a chador and took her away. Farhana tried to say something, but Ashfaq Khan's gaze was enough to keep her quiet.

* * *

'Uncle Ashfaq, you shouldn't have brought me here. It is not my place to live with you in a hujra.'

'My child, there is enough space here and plenty to eat and drink. You don't need to worry.'

'Uncle Ashfaq, in a matter of one hour I have become so poor that I don't even have parents. What did I do to deserve this?'

'My child, you bear no blame in this episode.'

'Why did Baba forsake me? Is he not my father? Is Naheed not my mother?'

'Put your mind to rest, child. We will discuss it later.'

'Is it a sin to get married of one's own will?'

'No, my child. It has never been a sin and shall never be so.'

'Then why did they blame me?'

'Let them say whatever they want to.'

'Now don't you worry about anything. From today onwards, you will bear my name. You will be my daughter.'

It is said that the chinar dried up in a single night. Ashfaq Khan was heard to have commented, 'The tears of Nazo dried up the chinar.' He then looked up towards the sky: 'Naheed and Saleem Khan, the Almighty will punish you severely for this.'

4

The Sage

The banyan tree provided an aura of holiness to Khan Sahib's hujra. Reverentially placed in the centre of the courtyard, rooms were built around it in a rectangle. Over years its branches had grown to cover the entire courtyard, providing shade to all who chose to sit under its calm presence. The veneration associated with this tree attracted both life and death. While some chose to construct a temporal complex around it like the hujra, elsewhere, others desired to be interred into their spiritual abode underneath the cool shade of its evergreen leaves.

Khan Sahib's hujra was considered the central point of Charbagh. Disputes and issues would be brought up to him for his wise intervention. For generations, the lone banyan tree had been witness to issues that were resolved amicably under it. Now, with Khan Sahib restricted to his bed, the mantle was worn by his brother-in-law, Ashfaq Khan, who was a permanent fixture at the hujra. Ashfaq Khan's philosophical take on practical issues brought up to him discouraged some from seeking his advice. While Khan Sahib had sought opportunities to utilize complaints to his advantage, Ashfaq Khan's approach was selfless. Believing ethics to be at the core of most of the issues, Ashfaq Khan's advice usually centred on asking the complainants to redirect their moral compass. His honest disposition had earned him a loyal circle of admirers, of which the outer circle comprised those who found amusement in his trenchant inquisition and sense of humour. On a typical evening, Ashfaq Khan would be found sitting under the banyan tree in dialogue with the village folk. He refused to consider anything sacrosanct, questioning rigid beliefs. An avuncular figure, popularly referred to as the wise man of Charbagh, people did not seem to mind his amusing inquisition, or so he believed.

Ashfaq Khan was one of those uniquely gifted men who saw and brought out the best in people. He took pride in identifying himself with the ordinary village folk and treated everyone with equal respect. His simple disposition, long, clean-shaven face and the formidable hair on his ears made him distinctly prominent. In a not-so-distant past, he had taught at the local school. With no personal ambition, he had got along well with everyone, providing his fellow teachers all the support they required, which usually meant filling in for them during their frequent leaves. It was his ambition to help the children transform their mindset from their narrow focus on learning for commercial reasons. But soon he realized it was the parents of these children who needed to be convinced. Despite the odds, he kept trying till he realized it was time for someone else to take over the task. He then confined himself to the hujra, defining his role as a local consultant. He would write letters for the uneducated, advise them on trivial matters and travel with them on short notice to the courts to engage with lawyers. And, in the evenings, he exchanged views with the locals, animating the dull life of the village.

* * *

As a boy, Abdul Aziz, the imam of Sher Zaman's new mosque, had the privilege of attending some of these sessions. What he distinctly remembered was the uneasiness his father felt in Ashfaq Khan's presence. He could not remember the discussions, but his father's hopeless incapacity to carry out a religious discussion, which always ended up in amusement for the listeners, was imprinted in his mind. He distinctly remembered his father's flushed face and his evident unease. Once they left the hujra, Khushrang would tell Abdul Aziz how the promptings of the devil led wise men astray. All his young mind could infer at the time was that people with ears covered with bountiful hair were not destined to hear the whispering of angels reserved for the pious. But that was a long time ago, and now armed with his own mosque and a pulpit, he wanted to take a fresh look at Ashfaq Khan's ears.

With a chador flung over his left shoulder, a white skullcap and a holy scowl, Abdul Aziz entered the hujra through its large green door, duly escorted by two boys. The cordiality of the initial conversation was as anticipated. Since Abdul Aziz was meeting Ashfaq Khan after a long time, he gave a highly opinionated summary of his life, replete with his achievements in a dramatic style, as if addressing a congregation. Ashfaq Khan kept picking up words from his sentences and repeating them for more explanation. It was only when Abdul Aziz had finished that he felt the need to say something about himself.

'Yes, here I am as happy as I was in my youth, under no pressure to prove anything and no fear of losing anything. The only item of complexity in my entire self is now my hearing aid, which fortunately no one can see because of my hair. I eat and drink, and thank Allah for blessing me with a gratified heart.'

The conversation continued and when the name of Khushrang was mentioned, Ashfaq Khan remarked, 'Your father was a kind-hearted man, but then Khan Sahib made him the imam of his mosque.'

'So, I presume he became even better,' Abdul Aziz tried to complete his sentence.

'Well, once he got into that profession, initially he became judgemental and later a misanthrope, all in the name of love for religion.'

As Abdul Aziz looked askance at Ashfaq Khan, he explained: 'How can you nurture hate when you profess love for the Creator five times a day?'

Abdul Aziz changed the topic, and they started talking about how the village had grown over the years. They also talked about the tendency among young men to leave the village for better prospects in the cities. To Abdul Aziz's remark about lack of employment opportunities, Ashfaq Khan commented, 'But you have been lucky to find a safe profession for yourself, isn't it?'

'This is not a profession, Khanji. This is a duty that Allah gives to some of His people.'

'Yes, but did you take it up by choice?'

'Yes, I did and so did my father,' Abdul Aziz said, looking straight into his eyes.

Ashfaq Khan smiled meaningfully, narrowing his eyes as Abdul Aziz's past flashed in his mind. Khushrang had tried his best to keep Abdul Aziz in school, but in vain. The boy would always find some legitimate excuse to leave during classes. Fed up with him, he had requested Ashfaq Khan to take him into his personal care, who had soon realized the gifted complexity. Abdul Aziz was highly intelligent but had low attention span accompanied by extreme mood swings. His chaotic mind made him jump from one thing to the other, sacrificing all forms of logical relationships. When Ashfaq Khan tried subjecting him to yogic concentration techniques, he burst out laughing. The boy was simply unmanageable. Nonetheless, he kept trying, considering him a project to be delivered to the village in the form of a refined young man. But Khushrang's physical abuse of his son made matters worse. There would be times when poor Abdul Aziz would keep sniffling for hours in Ashfaq Khan's office, while the other boys attended classes. The next day, to his surprise, Abdul Aziz would be a changed person altogether, targeting a peer for physical abuse. Ashfaq Khan tried speaking with Khushrang a few times but without success. Finally, the school management asked Khushrang to take Abdul Aziz away and put the fear of God into him. This he did by putting him into a small madrasa in the adjoining village, before asking for Sher Zaman's financial help to enrol him at the more prestigious one in Rawalpindi. With this background, Abdul Aziz still had the audacity to contradict Ashfaq Khan.

After a pause, Ashfaq Khan continued, 'It is good to have certainty in life. But in your case, there is a problem. The knowledge imparted to you in a madrasa starts with certainty and ends in certainty, squeezing out all forms of thought.'

Instead of responding further, Abdul Aziz thought it was safe to leave. It was seemingly a pleasant departure, but Ashfaq Khan's remarks had deeply hurt Abdul Aziz. He strongly felt that Ashfaq Khan had denigrated him as well as his father.

Over the next few months, Abdul Aziz and Ashfaq Khan met occasionally. Ashfaq Khan would usually indulge him in a conversation by asking him questions like, 'Maulana, don't you get tired talking about the same sins over and over again? Human creativity is so bankrupt, isn't it, Maulana; humans cannot even invent new sins.'

On other occasions he would ask, 'So, Maulana, I have heard that you have included a long list of sins to the existing ones your father preached about? But have you ever wondered, why do men sin in the first place?'

In Ashfaq Khan's presence, Abdul Aziz felt just like his father had: religiously bankrupt at the barrage of seemingly innocuous questions. He had never been exposed to this line of questioning. After his graduation, he had never felt the need to re-examine his convictions. His conclusions had taken firm roots even before he started his studies at the madrasa; the eight years were spent in cementing them. And after leaving the madrasa, he had never felt the need to consult his books.

Meanwhile, Ashfaq Khan's verbal assaults continued: 'So, Maulana, if our sins have remained the same over thousands of years, why do we need a priest to remind us of them?'

Abdul Aziz would frown but keep his head lowered. After a very long time he had met someone who had the audacity to humiliate him and that too in front of the ordinary village folk.

In his Friday sermons, Abdul Aziz usually highlighted the depravity of the Muslim world. He condemned music and dance to the fullest. The lone family of musicians still residing in the village felt threatened, and they asked Ashfaq Khan for help.

Abdul Aziz was adamant when Ashfaq Khan asked him not to pinpoint the poor family in his sermons.

'Yes, they may live among us, but they should change their profession,' was Abdul Aziz's firm reply.

'Tell me, Maulana, can you become a musician now?'

'Allah be praised, Khanji. May He keep me away from the works of the devil. As far as they are concerned, they can work on a farm.'

'And who will give them land to cultivate?'

'They don't need their own land. They can work as labourers. Khanji, how can you support this evil?'

* * *

These verbal exchanges happened every time they met. Meanwhile, Abdul Aziz's vociferous sermons were winning him a large audience. With a deep voice perfectly suited to convey the wrath of God, his emotionally charged oratory was creating an indelible impression on the dull minds of Charbagh. Naturally gifted with repartee and raw humour, he would crack the coarsest of jokes in the garb of religion, without facing any objection. He rebuked his audience for their unholy lives and despicable sins, declaring these to be the reasons at the core of the Muslim *ummah*'s current plight. The only way to redeem themselves was by closely associating with his mosque, which meant contributing more than they ever did towards the holy institution. His teaching was akin to the once prevalent concept of indulgence in Catholicism, whereby charity to the clergy formed the only legitimate way for redemption.

To gain prominence and further legitimize his point of view, Abdul Aziz invited a group of senior clerics from his alma mater to visit Charbagh. With no other decent place available, they had to stay at the hujra, which Ashfaq Khan was pleased to let out to the pious guests.

On the day of their arrival, after their engagements at the mosque, they came to the hujra to stay the night. Ashfaq Khan was in the courtyard, rolling up his prayer mat.

'Khanji, why do you pray alone? Why don't you come to the mosque?' Abdul Aziz asked after they had settled down into charpoys.

'Abdul Aziz, do you know it was for your sake that I stopped coming to the mosque?'

'My sake?'

'Yes, yours. One day, as a young boy, you came to the mosque looking for your father. When you saw him, you ran up to him and hugged him while he was leading the prayers. After he had finished, he beat you up ruthlessly for diverting his attention from the Universal to something as menial as yourself. I was the one who caught his hand and didn't let him complete the ritual to this heart's content. You must have been three or four at the time. That day I realized that I needed an alternate place for my spiritual levitation.'

As Abdul Aziz lowered his gaze, Ashfaq Khan addressed the visitors, 'Maulanas, you must have had a long day. I have arranged a musical evening for you.' He then introduced the three young men present as the rabab player, the tabla player and the singer. He eulogized the rabab player for his string control, the tabla player for his remarkable skill in changing the tempo of the song through his drums, and the singer for having the most poetically rhythmic choice of tappas.

'These boys form the best musical group in the entire district. Apart from love themes, their poetry carries the essence of hundreds of years of experience of the people of these lands. Ever since Abdul Aziz launched his war against these poor folk, I have asked them to perform regularly at the hujra so that they make some income.'

The maulanas didn't know how to respond to the situation. The only excuse they could come up with was that they had had a long day and would like to rest. So, they retired to their rooms, leaving Ashfaq Khan to enjoy the music.

The next evening, after Asr prayers, another discussion took place at the hujra. The topic under scrutiny was the mandatory sighting of the moon, especially for the holy month of Ramadan.

'Sighting of the moon is not a religious question,' Ashfaq Khan said seriously but the maulanas laughed it off as a joke. Only when Ashfaq Khan started explaining did they realize that an important realm of their authority was being pulled from under their feet. 'How can the movement of stars and planets form the purview of religion? Tell me, maulanas, do you ever say your prayers by consulting your watch? Do you ever confirm the movement of the sun to say your prayers? If you don't, then why do you insist on seeing the moon through the naked eye?'

The devout group was visibly offended, especially when they overheard some villagers agreeing with Ashfaq Khan's observations. The topic was skilfully diverted, but they were not to be let off so easily. After the night prayers, another discussion was held, in which Ashfaq Khan engaged them in a catechism of the worst kind.

'Maulanas, do you believe sin arises from vice or from virtue?'

'Ashfaq Khan, how can sin arise from virtue?' they asked in amazement.

'The sin arising from virtue is mutative and darker than the one arising from sin. Let me explain. There are people who are not spiritually qualified to interpret the book of Allah. One has to have a minimum level of spiritual cleanliness to read and understand the Quran.'

'What is that supposed to mean?'

'There is nothing more unfortunate than the desire to grab power behind religion. Veiled behind virtue are wicked intentions that give rise to the most unspeakable sins.'

Abdul Aziz, who was accompanying the group, was visibly offended. 'Ashfaq Khan, we must not revile the sanctity of the mosque and its defenders.'

'Do not take it personally, gentlemen. I am just stating a fact. In all times and ages, it has been difficult to find priests with consciences.'

If Ashfaq Khan thought it was the end of another discussion, he was wrong. This conversation was to form the basis of the future set-up of the village. In the past it was Abdul Aziz's father who would leave the hujra in a huff; now it was Abdul Aziz who felt humiliated by Ashfaq Khan's dialectic. But this time, Ashfaq Khan had misread the reaction of the younger generation to his harmless, philosophical exchange.

This generation of alpha clerics was mindful of its standing in society. Their teachers had spent their lives in poverty and enforced self-denial, only to be laughed upon and made to live on the hinterlands of society. Commonly referred to as mullah, a denigration of the word maulana, they were despised covertly across all segments. They were largely dependent on donations, and as a result were mocked at in local proverbs and idioms for their voracious eating habits and aversion to hard work. They were respectfully confined to the mosques and expected to carry out the ritualistic part of religion only. There were some among the clergy who would time and again remind the society of their presence, only to stand down after being given their due. But the world had changed, with people demanding more freedom and independence. For religion to enjoy the same, it was time to snatch the reins of the mosque from the powers that ran it from afar. No longer would the mosques be dependent on the charity of the landed aristocracy. Children studying at madrasas would no longer be seen going from house to house asking for food. Armed with the new reality, it was time to take revenge from the hypocritical society they had lived in for so long.

Ashfaq Khan's exchange with the maulanas had taken place just before the Nazo affair. Now that she was living with him in the hujra, she felt it was her place to point out his mistake. Her eyes brimmed with tears when she warned him, 'All of them will now gang up against you and make us leave this place.' But Ashfaq Khan replied with a smile, reassuring her that there was nothing to worry about.

* * *

Ever since Ashfaq Khan had taken custody of Nazo, both Saleem and Sher Zaman had stopped going to the hujra. They didn't want to be lectured by Ashfaq Khan over their gross misconduct towards Nazo. Although she was confined to the room she was assigned, the villagers strongly disapproved of the desecration of the traditional Pukhtoon institution of hujra.

Even before the Nazo affair, Saleem and Sher Zaman hadn't been too sure of Ashfaq Khan's utility to them. Each had tried to pull him towards himself, but, to their disappointment, instead of supporting one or the other in their quest for reallocation of land, he had supported the clichéd cause of justice, antagonizing both. And after the Nazo affair, they didn't have the moral courage to face him. In addition to this, with Khan Sahib's health deteriorating, he had become the virtual owner of the hujra, where a section of villagers still valued his advice as it was based on honesty.

Meanwhile, Abdul Rehman, the younger brother of Abdul Aziz, had taken charge of Khan Sahib's mosque after his father's death. This young man was of feeble nature and lacked the understanding of what was expected of him. Saleem could not have found a better candidate for the family's mosque. He had followed Khan Sahib's lead by appointing another half-priest as imam.

With both the mosques under Abdul Aziz's control, he immediately targeted higher income as his objective. The specific source Abdul Aziz wanted to divert to himself was the sale of hides of sacrificial animals that were collected during Eid al-Adha. For years, villagers had donated these hides to Ashfaq Khan for supporting the families of the unprivileged, who had enrolled their children in the local school. This income took care of their fees and other expenses of the families as well. If only Abdul Aziz could divert these hides to his mosque, he would become more independent. He sincerely believed the day was not far when all mosques in the country would regain the glory of yesteryears by generating their own income, instead of being dependent on charity. He had laid down his ambition to the group of scholars he had invited, who in return had endorsed his point of view, praising him for his noble objective.

* * *

Ashfaq Khan had seriously underestimated Abdul Aziz and the clergy. The Friday after the scholars left, rumour was that some important announcement would be made from the pulpit. Khan's men were seen speaking to people in the streets, pointing out the acrimonious exchanges that had taken place between an irreverent Ashfaq Khan and the scholars. Even before that, all kind of rumours had been spread about him and Nazo, with the intention of creating repulsion. Ashfaq Khan knew everything but had kept quiet. The number of visitors to the hujra had decreased considerably, giving him more time to spend with his books and looking after Nazo.

The Friday sermon by Abdul Aziz was vociferous and full of invective. His dusky face was black with emotion as he denounced the depravity of the Pukhtoons, which he believed was based on rabab and kabab. Once he was finished with the denunciation of the entire race, without mincing any words, he went straight for Ashfaq Khan. Brazenly taking his name, to the shock of many, he pointedly disparaged him for the clandestine role he was playing against religion by utilizing the sanctity of a hujra. He denounced the people who visited the hujra and enjoyed his company. And then he mocked him by saying, 'And to top it all, now he has the audacity to start living with a young unrelated girl, masquerading as her father. How can this village witness the breaking of Allah's laws with such impunity? Is there not a single honourable Muslim left to stop this depravity?' As Abdul Aziz thundered, he was pleased to see the response he got. Unfortunately for Ashfaq Khan, his unconventional thoughts and absence from the mosque, provided them ample ammunition. Abdul Aziz knew he could use the pulpit to his advantage; sacred scorn heaped from this position could neither be defended nor repulsed. Every word coming out of that microphone was attributed to the will and pleasure of Allah. Ashfaq Khan was demonized as an instrument planted by unknown powers bent on destroying the remaining glory of a perfect religion. And so his tirade, like his father's against the zindiqs at one time, took such hateful discourse that by the time he had finished, Ashfaq Khan and his like were firmly believed to be the supporters of shaitan.

With Abdul Aziz and the Khan brothers up in arms against Ashfaq Khan, he didn't stand much chance. As emotions reached a boiling point, an enraged crowd decided to storm the hujra immediately after the prayers. They weren't too sure about Ashfaq Khan's fault but only what they had been told by Abdul Aziz and the supporters of the two Khans; it was in defence of their faith and religion. They did not need instructions about the treatment to be meted out to Ashfaq Khan. The poor village folk carried volumes of inflammable emotion, available for discharge at the slightest provocation. This was the younger generation of the same people who had carried out a similar verdict some three decades ago. On that day, Khushrang's invective had succeeded in mobilizing a large crowd, who had run amok through the streets, attacking the houses of the zindiqs. The unlucky ones were pulled out of their houses and beaten to death in the narrow alleys. Nobody had cared to listen to their pleas. Ten people lost their lives and five houses were burnt down. Later, the same houses were justly divided by Khan Sahib among the people of the village. As this highly charged group reached the gate of the hujra, a man came running from behind shouting at the top of his voice: 'Khan Sahib has passed away!'

* * *

Immaculately dressed in white with a matching Pukhtoon cap, Ashfaq Khan slowly emerged from his room with Nazo close behind him. Her face was fully covered, and she had a red dotted chador wrapped tightly around her. Carrying a sombre look, Ashfaq Khan crept towards the hujra door. Holding the Holy Quran firmly to his chest with his left hand and his walking stick in his right, he kept mumbling prayers. He then stopped, nodded in acknowledgement at the servants who bowed as he and Nazo left the village, perhaps for the last time.

'Where are we headed, Baba?' Nazo asked as she sat in the car. On the third day after Khan Sahib's death, Ashfaq Khan had asked Nazo to pack up her things, without telling her about their destination.

'My child, why worry? Allah hasn't forsaken us. He will take care of us.'

'Yes, He will, but how? We don't even have a place to go to.'

'Stop looking so worried. If you ask me, I am only worried about my book collection. I have asked Lala's son to send them to me at the earliest. It's my treasure, which I hope you will take care of one day.'

'Baba, will we be able to leave the village?'

'My child, we just walked through the village to reach the car.'

'But where are we going?'

'My child, even a loner like me has a trick up his sleeve. After Khan Sahib fell ill, I managed to get a small flat for myself in Islamabad.' Through her tearful eyes, Nazo beheld Ashfaq Khan's triumphant smile.

5

The Blasphemer

The faculty and staff were in awe of the young English literature lecturer, Junaid. After all, he had survived an air crash in a Christian country and was the sole survivor. Allah be praised, he must have been chosen for a greater task on this planet! It was a perplexing scenario. A student of English literature, who had obtained a master's degree from the University of Edinburgh, had been chosen for some divine purpose! And, on top of that, he was the sole survivor! It would have been understandable if he was an Islamic theology student, but for nature to preserve someone like Junaid—a beardless, non-practising Muslim—was one of the mysteries of Allah they were unable to comprehend. Flying from one godless town to another—Inverness to Edinburgh—wasn't an odyssey the Islamic angels would worry about; but to have identified him for survival required deeper analysis.

Junaid's presence on the campus of the University of Kohat invoked heated discussions between the various groups of students and faculty about nature's prudence in his survival. They held different opinions about him: some said the prayers of his mother were the sole reason while others dismissed it as a chance occurrence. His survival could not be classified under any of the various subsets of fate, prompting some to seek the advice of the maulanas of the local Darul Uloom. In the town of Kohat, located in the province of Khyber Pakhtunkhwa, people routinely turned to the clergy for determining the will and pleasure of Allah. It may be added that before the establishment of the University of Kohat, this reputable madrasa had served the masses for dissemination of knowledge. This labour of love, in its seventy years of existence, had, by now, converted into a sectarian-based institution. The madrasa board narrowed down these broad discussions to a single question: Whether by saving Junaid, Allah had acted out of discretion or out of mercy? Even then there was a clear split: one group was adamant on attributing his survival to Allah's mercy while the other was bent on proving His discretion. Nevertheless, despite all these discussions and catechisms, a definitive resolution could not be reached. Meanwhile, Junaid continued living among them as nature's riddle and could not understand the looks he received from everyone.

Junaid was one of those students who had been inspired by the polemics of Ashfaq Khan. While studying at the high school in Charbagh, he had always looked forward to the weekly after-class discussions. Ashfaq Khan had taken this initiative for the ninth and tenth grade students. He would, in his characteristic style, pull up a chair and initiate the discussion by putting a question to them. Participation in these dialogues was entirely voluntary. All comments were considered relevant, and no one was ever ridiculed. Adopting the Socratic model, he thoroughly analysed every statement made by the participants. Students dreaded the follow-up questions as he pushed them to defend their point of view. All he wanted was for them to make use of their minds, rationally and without any bias. Ashfaq Khan's incisive wit made the discussions lively for those who enjoyed such polemics. He strongly believed in exercising the mind first before reading the coursebooks. 'A book cannot harm a dull mind,' he would say. These boys, he believed, were just at the right age to get on to the thinking track. Once that was accomplished, no force could ever derail them again.

Despite Ashfaq Khan's best efforts, every year, hardly one-third of the class participated in these sessions. It was Junaid, however, who always looked forward to them. He towered above all others in objectivity, content and articulation. His humble background—his father had a small shop in the village—didn't make him conscious or stop him from expressing his opinions. After the other students left, Junaid tended to stay back and request further discussion on the topic. Ashfaq Khan would take off his glasses, smile at the enthusiastic young man and entertain his passionate discourse. He was happy to see that Junaid could pick relatively obscure points from the discussion, which were seldom noticed by others. Ashfaq Khan firmly believed that if Junaid continued his studies, he would make a positive contribution to society.

Junaid was in the final semester of his master's in English when Ashfaq Khan was forced to leave the village. When he came to know about it, Ashfaq Khan had already left, and the gloom of irrationality hung over the village. For hours, Junaid contemplated the two years of weekly sessions he had attended. Although these classes were of no help in the compulsory subjects, they had given him the perspective to question the veracity of established facts. While he could not question the deductive methodology of science—and had to accept the facts as presented—his acquired propensity to define the objective of each exercise helped him rationally interpret the given text. This structured thinking had helped him with all the subjects.

From an early age, Junaid had shown deep interest in languages. Ashfaq Khan was pleasantly surprised to find him holding the book of an Urdu author during one of the weekly sessions. From that time on, he had personally guided him by recommending and often buying him books of classical literature in both English and Urdu. The best part was that Junaid not only read them but marked them and wrote his comments in the margins. He remembered once showing a heavily marked book by an English author to Ashfaq Khan. 'A book that does not inspire a single mark is an utter disrespect to the author,' Ashfaq Khan had said with a smile.

Junaid's sheer intellect and willpower made him stick to his studies in the worst of monetary circumstances. He started making the most use of the regular scholarships he received without bothering his poor father for money. Fate smiled upon him when he was awarded a scholarship to pursue a master's degree at the University of Edinburgh.

* * *

On weekends, to make the best use of the Scottish summer, Junaid would take a book with him to read in the Castle gardens. Running along the entire length of Princes Street, these gardens were a favourite among locals and tourists alike. He preferred a bench just behind the Scott Monument. To add to the pleasure, he would buy coffee from Patisserie Valerie on the North Bridge.

It was absolute bliss to read while sipping coffee in these lush green gardens. He had come a long way—from the village of Charbagh to the University of Peshawar and now here. Life had been rewarding, and he was thankful to the Almighty for giving him the one-year scholarship for his master's degree in English literature. He would often look up at the sky and say, 'Thank you, Allah, for everything' before returning to the pleasure of the written word.

Junaid's one-year sojourn in Edinburgh introduced him to the various facets of Western society. For the first time he saw and appreciated the liberty enjoyed by both sexes. Freedom of thought and action in the university were exactly as he had imagined. Students were free to comment on anything without the fear of repercussions. And the best part was that no one seemed to notice his wheatish complexion, his sunken eyes and protruding cheeks. While the Scottish society, like many others, still hadn't outgrown its bias in favour of body shaming, it was done discreetly, without any provocation. The intrusive questions were limited to which country he came from and if he was married. Apart from that, neither the university nor the students cared about his beliefs or habits. No one ever asked him if he went to a church or a mosque. Therefore, he was pleasantly surprised when he visited the main mosque just behind the Royal Mile and met some equally non-intrusive people. These smiling Muslims were a pleasant change from the sombre-looking religious figures he was used to in his country. But the greatest discovery for him was the ease with which the Western society ran its affairs without invoking any deity. No one ever used the word Inshallah or its equivalent and still managed to reach their goals. So, he decided to stay back for another year and look more deeply into the philosophical paradigms of the East and the West. By the end of the second year, he had obtained a master's degree in Philosophy, with a major in Islamic thought.

During the process of synthesizing the two philosophies, Junaid, along with a group of friends, decided to visit Inverness, the capital of the Scottish Highlands. The group decided to fly back to Edinburgh. The journey was too short to arouse any divine interest, but it so happened that the twenty-seven people on the plane were destined to face a tragedy. The plane got caught in a storm and eventually crashed, killing everyone on board, except Junaid. They later told him that he was miraculously thrown out of the plane into a field. Junaid made headlines around the world because he had received just minor injuries.

Junaid spent the ensuing few months, until the end of his master's degree in Philosophy, in a stupor. During this time, he attended classes, studied for his exams and submitted his dissertation. Even when he came back to his own country, it took him time to overcome the shock of the accident. The faces of his friends who perished in the accident would pop up out of nowhere, disconnecting him from his surroundings. He would fall into deep thought, contemplating the meaning of the tragedy. As he recovered slowly, he often joked that the barley from the field he was thrown into was used to make the best Scotch whisky in the world.

Junaid had always wanted to become a teacher. The government scholarship awarded to him stipulated that he come back and teach at the appointed university for at least five years. He would have preferred Peshawar, but he wasn't given a choice and was asked to join the University of Kohat.

* * *

By the looks of the faculty and students, Junaid realized he had entered a madrasa—in its common parlance. As his interactions increased, he realized that theology dominated all the departments, especially the English. His colleagues were grumpy old men, who read out their notes to the class, expecting the students to regurgitate the same in their exams. The notes seemed to be scribbled on parchments. The thought of revising the curriculum had not occurred to the authorities, making these notes as relevant as they were thirty years ago.

To Junaid's horror, there were hardly any discussions that took place in class. Even if they did, they were carried out in Pushto, the local language. So, when he started insisting that the students speak only English, they thought he was being boastful about his proficiency. On his part, he wanted to rid them of their shyness by putting in an effort to speak the language, but soon realized their limited level. Almost half the students in his class were female.

They had their chadors wrapped tightly around them in the hope of blocking out all external influence and were not expected to take any active part in class. Therefore, it created quite a stir when he tried to open up the floor for discussion and encouraged them to participate as well. Some boys attributed this encouragement to traces of depravity. Although Junaid came from the same background as them— he was from the same province and spoke the same language—the grooming imparted by Ashfaq Khan and his own experiences had helped rip off the veneer of false conservatism from his mind.

Despite frequent reminders from his head of department, he just couldn't stick to the given course. While explaining a certain chapter, he would take his students straight into English homes to make them empathize with the protagonists, without being judgemental. He made them roam the moors and plough the fields; he made them enter the church to see the Christian rituals. Junaid's teaching method aimed at vicarious interpretation of text: to make his students feel and equate the sanctity of tears shed in a mosque to the tears shed in a church.

'These stories from a foreign land are of people who are like us,' he would say. 'They are equally honourable, equally dignified and equally courageous. They carry the same aspirations, and in achieving them, they suffer from the same weaknesses that we do.' Junaid's emphatic lectures were impressive but raised eyebrows. How could he equate Muslim piety with Christian devotion?

And, to top it all, he decided to start showing the class a movie based on some classic every week. As a start, he showed them the adaptation of *Far from the Madding Crowd*, a classic by Thomas Hardy.

* * *

Mr Zareen Khan, the perpetually brooding head of the English department, sat across the table. With his head slightly bent and eyebrows arched, he had to look over his pince-nez when talking to someone across the table. Sitting in his own room, he had the discretion to take off his glasses for a more humane interaction. But, perhaps, he thought his current posture was more formidable, giving him greater leverage over his addressee. With a large gulp of the saliva that seemed to have accumulated during the time he took to stare Junaid down, he took a deep breath indicative of something unpleasant to be conveyed.

'Mr Junaid, we have received complaints that the movie you showed the class on the weekend was not appropriate, and it has deeply hurt the religious and cultural sentiments of the students.'

'Sir, I just showed them the classic *Far from the Madding Crowd*.'

'I know. Perhaps you need some time to culturally assimilate yourself with the environment.'

'Sir, I belong to this province, and I fully understand the sensitivities of my people.'

'In that case, you shouldn't have shown the movie.'

Junaid kept wondering if the blue-eyed Julie Christie had evoked a belated satanic impulse. No one from the class had complained during or even after the movie. In fact, he had held a detailed discussion with them on the various characters the next working day.

However, Zareen Khan objected to Junaid's teaching method as well. He advised him to stick to the course and not sidetrack into other branches of knowledge. Junaid tried to explain the steps he was taking to bring up level of understanding of the students and improve their verbal skills. While he spoke, he saw Zareen Khan stifle his yawn a couple of times. When he had finished, Zareen Khan leaned back and said, 'Junaid sahib, we are here to teach the language; we do not need to empathize with any culture. You see, empathy is the first step in accepting foreign culture. We are deeply religious in this university and would like to keep it as such. Let us keep our learning limited to the language.'

* * *

Junaid's proficiency of the language and his eloquence attracted students to his class. The dull and repetitive reading from yellow parchments was replaced by genuine lectures. Junaid did not need to refer to a book or a text when he lectured. He always came prepared and passionately explained the context behind a chapter or a poem. While he was slowly becoming a celebrity in his own right, his colleagues in the English department were not too pleased with his performance. In private, they accused him of being a liberal—a broadly defined term for non-practising Muslims. A small number of students—associated with a religious political party—also started to take note of his lectures and activities.

Junaid did not take the discussion with the head of the department as a warning. In his academic innocence, he did not seem to care about what was brewing against him. His energy centred on his students. In his myopic zeal to bring up the level of his students, he started adding texts from sources that were considered profane in religious circles. As time progressed, Junaid kept absorbing intellectual shocks.

In one of the classes, a student rudely contradicted him as he spoke about the mysteries of the universe. 'Sir, as per our religious belief, the earth doesn't rotate, it remains static.'

Junaid couldn't believe his ears. As he looked around, he realized that the student was not cracking a joke. The religious leanings of the majority of the class were skewed in favour of this doctrine; and in case they weren't, they chose not to contradict the student. Junaid couldn't resist arguing with him. By the end, he got so worked up that he walked out of the classroom.

On another occasion, he saw a student constantly whispering. As he walked up to him, he realized that he was counting the beads of the *tasbeeh* in his hand.

'Shahzad,' Junaid looked at him intently, 'I wonder if this is the right time for you to do your *wazeefa*.'

'Sir, we should never let ourselves forget Allah,' was the determined answer he received.

'But you won't be able to concentrate.'

'Sir, if Allah wills, I will do better than others,' was his reply.

Junaid had genuine sympathizers among his students, who constantly advised him not to provoke the religious-minded people. But Junaid did not understand their point of view. He was focused on trying to expand the mental horizons of his students, without realizing the unprepared state of his audience. This time it resulted in a departmental inquiry against him.

* * *

Two other professors from the English department assisted Zareen Khan in the inquisition. Junaid had three allegations against him: that he frequently quoted from Abul Ala Al Maari, a known sceptic in the traditional Islamic traditions; that he publicly denounced Imam Al Ghazali's treatise on cause and effect; and that he believed in free will.

Junaid's response to the committee was passionate and knowledgeable: Yes, I have quoted from Al

Maari; but what was wrong with the quotations? The insight of a sceptic might not compare with a hundred years of dull piety of a conformist. What is more pious? Tell me, Sirs? Frequenting the Kaaba with ill-gotten wealth, expecting to hoodwink the angels? That is what Al Maari refers to in the text that I quoted in class, and the one that I have been complained against.'

He added, 'And as for the theory of cause and effect by Al Ghazali, well, it should never be taught by the uneducated to the young minds. We live in the world of cause and effect. Every action has to have a reaction.'

One of the professors interrupted, 'Junaid sahib, do not forget that you survived a crash. By your logic, you should be dead. In fact, it reinforces Ghazali's concept of cause being unrelated to effect.'

'Sir, I have never repudiated Ghazali's point of view in toto. I agree with his logic to the extent of proving the claim for miracles associated with prophets. Yes, I survived the crash by Allah's will. If you dissociate cause from effect, what are you left with? Let us then say goodbye to all the scientific endeavours and burn our books.

'With regards to free will, how can anyone lecture me on that? As pointed out, I survived a plane crash—in fact, I was the only survivor. My life was predestined, but I will be judged on my free will. Isn't it, Sirs? Won't I be judged on my free will, or will I be forgiven for the plane crash? The truth for me as an individual is in my free will. My predestination has played its part in the form of the air crash.'

The inquiry at the university was promptly reported to the madrasa authorities. A denunciation was issued by the madrasa based on the minutes of the inquiry. A written warning was issued to Junaid, which read, 'We have been informed of your academic ventures which seem to lie outside your purview and your limited knowledge. Your critique of the established principles of Islamic thought is not appreciable. Given your ignorance of the Quran and the fact that you have not undertaken serious religious education, you must not digress into the realm of religion. If you want clarification of any matter pertaining to theology or jurisprudence, you may visit our madrasa. It is sincerely hoped that any further divergence will not take place. We pray for your guidance.'

Unfortunately, it was not to be, and despite his well-wishers pleading with him to not further agitate religious sensitivities, Junaid could not bring himself to follow the guidelines. When his sympathizers would ask him not to get into confrontations, his lean face would become sombre, and he would start staring at the floor.

'I love all my students. I love everyone in this university. In fact, I love all the students of the madrasa as well. If they don't open up their minds, they cannot make use of any knowledge. If they want to achieve the glory of yesteryears that they refer to, they need to embrace knowledge and wisdom.'

* * *

The straw that broke the camel's back was Junaid's comment on the requirement of religion for morality. In his nonchalant manner he declared, 'You don't need religion to teach morality. Humans can devise a set of moral values for themselves.'

As soon as he uttered these words, a radical student stood up and threatened him with dire consequences before leaving the class.

'How can you separate religion from morality? There is no morality without religion. You will not go unpunished. This time you have gone too far, Mr Junaid. We will teach you a lesson.'

As he stormed out, a few other students followed him, leaving Junaid bewildered.

* * *

'Sir, you must leave in my car. No, forget your belongings. Just take your wallet. A large crowd is on its way to lynch you,' one of his student admirers said urgently as soon as he entered Junaid's room.

'Sir, you have to be in the trunk. You must not be seen.'

As the car reached the university gate, it was obstructed by a large crowd of students chanting slogans against Junaid. 'Death to the blasphemer,' they shouted. The security guards obediently opened the gates and stood aside watching the charged students. The faculty and other university staff were nowhere to be seen. The crowd mobbed the car and pointedly asked the driver about the whereabouts of Junaid. Lying in the trunk, Junaid wasn't sure if he would be able to get away. This could be a trap. He would probably be delivered as a package directly to the instigators of this enterprise. But he couldn't do much except lie still and pray. He heard the slogans and for the first time in his life he felt scared. So, Allah had saved him from the plane crash to be lynched by a mob, he thought. Some of the agitators started banging the car's bonnet. It was just a matter of time before they opened the trunk and pulled him out. No one would dare come to his rescue. The verbal charge of blasphemy was enough for the mob to lynch him. He heard the ignition turn off; the driver seemed to have been pulled out of the car.

* * *

Ashfaq Khan couldn't control the tears flowing down his cheeks. Having grown a beard, his erudite look now carried a flavour of spirituality as well. For the past one hour, he had tried to talk to Junaid but in vain. An emaciated man, a shadow of the former Junaid, sat staring into the abyss. Gone was the glint in his eyes. It had been five years since he had been caught from his village, Charbagh. The police party had searched for him for over a month and finally on a tip-off had surrounded his home. Expecting intellectual salvos of the worst kind, a large posse, including heavily armed commandos, had taken part in the operation. They had called out to him on loudspeakers to surrender. It was ridiculous to ask an intellectual to come out with hands up in the air. Instead, they should have asked him to throw out his intellect into the street so they could shoot it.

First Information Report for blasphemy was registered against Junaid. It couldn't get worse. Once in jail, he had to be kept in solitary confinement. He was twice attacked by convicts serving life imprisonments for the worst crimes imaginable. Desperate to redeem their souls, they were certain to receive Divine grace by killing a blasphemer.

And the boy who had helped Junaid leave the university in his car was also indicted as an accomplice. Even though there was threat to his own life, he had not only helped Junaid escape the university but had also kept him in a safe house for over a month. However, Junaid couldn't have lived like that forever and had to leave for Charbagh.

The rollercoaster trial had taken its toll on Junaid. In the first year of the trial, his lawyer, the only courageous man in the province who had taken up the case, was shot dead by unknown assailants in his office. There was no one else willing to defend him. Junaid volunteered to plead his own case, but the technicalities were too much for him to handle. Every time he tried to make an argument, the army of plaintiffs would shoot it down on some technicality. Five years passed. Initially Junaid was optimistic. He was sure that Allah's mercy would help him leave the prison. But his suffering was predestined. A week prior to Ashfaq Khan's visit, the high court had declared him guilty of blasphemy. The sentence could be appealed in the Supreme Court, but there was very little chance that he would be declared innocent. Even if he were declared innocent, he could not live safely in any part of the country. Unfortunately, by this time, Junaid had lost his sanity. So when Ashfaq Khan showed up in a somewhat altered appearance, he shouted at him, 'Another one who calls me a blasphemer.' Ashfaq Khan tried his best to converse with Junaid, but soon realized it was of no use. When he started crying, Junaid burst out laughing. After the fit of laughter was over, he became still once again. After another long silence, Junaid got up and said, 'Now, if you will excuse me, I have a class to teach. Today I shall be discussing *Crime and Punishment*.' As the guard came in to ask Ashfaq Khan to leave, Junaid turned and addressed Ashfaq Khan, 'Predestination is more powerful than free will.'

6

The General's Son

The white letters of the word 'cafeteria' were fashioned in stark contrast to the dark asphalt pavement that marched up to it. From the enormous wrought-iron gate, the cafeteria seemed to be the only institution built under the wisdom of the air force. Once inside, the barracks, which had been zealously converted into classrooms, became visible. The institution was specifically founded for the children of the itinerant air force officers, whose disciplined flight path remained unassailable. The high walls around the PAF Degree College ensured the myth was kept a guarded secret, far from the prying eyes of bloody civilians.

This was among the few English-medium colleges in the country, designed to impart perpetual ignorance up to the level of bachelor's only. It was the only institution in the conservative city of Peshawar that allowed intermingling of sexes before the acceptable age of consent: master's degree. Civilian students did manage to get through, but only on the allocated quota and that too after they were thoroughly scanned for traces of perversion. Their ill-disciplined upbringing was considered unhealthy for the puritanical environment of the college associated with the armed forces.

In the Peshawar of the late 1970s and early 1980s, PAF Degree College was an anomaly. To cope with it, the environment was structured to limit interaction between boys and girls. However, a minuscule proportion, the adventurous kind, did manage to communicate across the demarcated line by exchanging notes. Segregation was strictly followed. Boys and girls had separate entrances to the cafeteria, and even the pavement was divided into separate walking lanes.

It was outrageous, therefore, when Akbar and Asma, first year FSc (fellow of science) students, decided to stare into the fiery eyes of tradition by sticking together both within and outside the class. Not just the college but the entire city was set ablaze by the scandal. Armed with religious texts, a large proportion of the society inveighed against co-education in the comfort of their living rooms, beating back those in favour of it. Heated exchanges took place between parents on the demerits of mixed gender education. Aware of the impact the scandal was having on the college and its reputation, the management issued an edict, making it compulsory for girls to start covering their heads.

It had been going on for a year: Akbar, the son of a senior air force officer, and Asma, the daughter of a businessman. Asma, the vivacious newcomer, was a local celebrity. Her fame was attributed to the expertise of the hairdresser who had given her the perfect Lady Diana hairstyle, earning her the same name. And those were the times when, with the Royal Wedding on the cards, Lady Diana had captured the imagination of the world. Her every style was being copied and every move scrutinized by the media. So, when boys from other colleges waited for hours to catch a glimpse of Asma, one did realize the star power of Lady Diana and the impact even her imitators had on their admirers. This dusky adolescent, whose mischievous kohl-lined eyes melted the hearts of many, was friendly yet reserved. She had the knack of bringing about a fashionable twist to something even as drab as a school uniform. While other girls wore their blue shirts with collars as limp as their beliefs, she wore hers straight, covering half her neck. The essential scarf was neatly pressed to form a V over her chest.

Despite her limited academic credentials, a handful of desperados would always be eager to borrow her notes, as a cover to their innocent intentions. One of them was rumoured to spend hours lying on his couch, with her notes on his chest. The others squirmed with desire, without having the confidence to accost her.

Akbar and Asma had got into an argument during an English class. Akbar, always convinced about his knowledge of everything, had found the novel *Goodbye, Mr Chips* horrendously outdated and irrelevant, while Asma believed it to be a fine piece of literature. Despite the teacher's intervention, neither budged from their stance and the argument became personal. This altercation somehow ended up forming a communication bridge between them, only to be crossed at a later stage. It was another girl, Annie, who acted as a catalyst, pushing both on to the bridge towards each other.

Annie came from one of the futuristic looking families of Peshawar. Her father served as a commander in the education corps of the air force and had lived a large part of his service years in foreign countries. Having interacted with people from diverse backgrounds, he had realized there were finer things to worry about than honour alone. A large collection of paintings by European masters adorned his house. For the uncultured, the main table of their drawing room carried a tome describing the artists and their paintings.

Annie had invited some of her female class-fellows to her birthday party. Now that she was in college, her father had agreed to let her invite a couple of *decent boys* as well. Ali and Akbar had made the cut. Ali and Akbar were friends and usually hung out together. The boys landed up together at Annie's place in Akbar's formidable Mazda Coupe 626. It was already the talk of the town and people yearned to see it. The girls were just entering Annie's place when the car pulled into the driveway. Initially Asma had casually glanced at the car, but while entering had turned around to look at it again.

Everyone was dressed to impress. Akbar, as always, was classy in his simple black trousers, cream-coloured shirt and a light-blue patterned scarf. A fashion icon of his college, Akbar had introduced the scarf instead of the school tie in the same colours. This novelty was so well-received that even the boys who were jealous of him had adopted it. And being the son of an influential father, the faculty found it safe not to interfere in these mundane matters of uniform.

It took some time for the group to relax and talk to each other. They became friendlier when they started playing charades. Akbar and Asma, despite being on opposite teams, seemed to get along pretty well. During a break in the activity, Ali went out into the lounge and started looking at the paintings. Annie followed him and asked him if he was enjoying the party. After some small talk, she asked him to wait for her in the lounge. She re-entered, accompanied by her father, whom she introduced to Ali. The interaction was limited to pleasantries and some basic questions all elders are supposed to ask students about career, etc. Her father then went back inside without going into the drawing room.

'My father has his work cut out for him after his retirement,' she said smilingly as soon as he had left. 'He intends to get engaged with Peshawar University for reassessing their various master's degree programmes.'

'So, when is he retiring?'

'In a year's time! And then we will move to Islamabad,' said Annie as they walked back into the drawing room.

Ali's heart sank.

Akbar and Asma were all smiles when they parted. They even waved at each other.

* * *

'So, you like Annie, don't you?' Akbar squinted his eyes and cast a sideways glance at Ali.

'And someone really made friends with Asma,' Ali retorted.

'I wish I could show you the smile on your face,' Akbar continued, ignoring Ali's remark. 'She was ravishing in white. A fair girl in a white dress! If only she were a little taller. But that is okay, I guess. You could always inject some growth hormones. Didn't I see you preen to get her attention? And then she introduced you to her father.'

Ali blushed. 'Even if I like her, there is not much I can do at this age. Need to get my degree first, find a job and . . .'

'And by that time, she will be married, loser!' Akbar completed his friend's sentence.

Ali was one of the few people Akbar was less suspicious about. His trust level with Ali had increased when, in one of the younger classes, he had stood up to an abrasive classmate who was hell-bent on ridiculing Akbar for his choice of glasses. From that time onwards, their friendship had progressively strengthened till the time Akbar's father became a man of consequence.

With limited places to visit in Peshawar, their rendezvous was Akbar's safe haven, where they would end up watching the latest Indian and English movies. The two were not the only ones who had fallen victim to the scourge of the VCR; the entire Pakistani Ummah had been taken in by this storm. With religion becoming more intrusive by the day, people could relax only in the privacy of their homes. The vociferous prayer leaders were quick to denounce it, asking people to keep their homes and hearths clean from this satanic invasion perpetrated by the Jewish and Christian lobbies against innocent Muslims. In fact, people were led to believe that entertainment was a conspiracy to destroy Islamic culture.

In the coming days, Ali noticed the smiles and furtive glances that Akbar and Asma exchanged but didn't think much of it. Akbar had found a muse and that was it, he thought. A couple of times Akbar did mention Asma and that they had spoken, but as a passing remark only. Ali didn't pay much attention. Akbar told Ali about the affair after a few months, albeit in his typical guarded manner. Ali didn't believe him at first. Once he realized that Akbar was serious, he tried to dissuade him, explaining the complications that could arise, but Akbar smiled in his nonchalant manner, dismissing his fears.

'You want me to stop loving her?'

'This is not love, Akbar.'

'Have you ever been in love?'

Ali kept quiet without taking the argument any further. A few months down the road, he realized that Akbar would not stop. He couldn't find a way to dissuade him from carrying on with the relationship, so he decided to stand by his friend. Even when the other boys would try to make fun of Akbar, Ali would respond with a stern expression, forcing them to back off.

The affair shook the pillars of tradition. Fearing he would pull his father's rank, college authorities did not ask Akbar to keep distance from Asma. To bring about a semblance of sanctity to the affair, Akbar and Asma asked Ali to hang out with them when they were in college. But Ali refused, saying that he did not intend to be a thorn between two flowers. But he never left Akbar; he stood by him. As they entered the last year of college, Akbar told Ali that he would soon be marrying Asma.

'My parents have finally agreed. It took me a while to convince my mother, but now she has also agreed.' Akbar's face lit up and his long eyelashes could not contain the twinkle in his light-brown eyes.

Akbar's mother was a formidable lady: a soft-spoken woman whose actions centred on protecting her family. She believed it was her right to get a teacher fired for scolding her daughter at PAF College or have a serving officer transferred for not providing due protocol during her visit to another city. All her decrees had to be carried out promptly. In all these years, Ali had met her only once at a dinner hosted on the great lawn of the Air House. Determined to keep her composure, she had acknowledged his greeting with a half nod and a cordial smile. She always liked to keep an aura of impermeability around the family. His father was, however, more forthcoming in his approach towards his son's best friend and had given him a tight hug.

Akbar continued, 'We will both go to the US and do our bachelor's there.' He seemed to have drawn out a plan already.

'But you are only eighteen? What is the hurry?'

'It is religiously recommended to get married as soon as one becomes an adult.' Akbar would stroke his hair with his fingers every time he made a religious argument.

'As if you are very religious; I have known you for seven years.'

Despite their friendship, Ali never inquired about the current status of their relationship. He left it entirely to Akbar's discretion to let him know the details.

* * *

Akbar's driver Aziz Sahib's duty was to take the cars
to the parking lot. According to the defined protocol
of Akbar's house, a car could not be left on the porch
and had to be promptly parked. Men of consequence
like Akbar's father needed to have different living
conventions. Aziz Sahib greeted Ali and the friend
whom he was seeing for the very first time. Wearing a
light moustache and copious hair, this new friend had
a scandalously proportioned stern; quite unusual for
a boy of that age; and the tightly fitted jeans caught
the imagination in a trap; a stare could not escape its
magnetism. As he hurriedly surveyed this newcomer,
he thought it must be the stress on the internal organs
that had caused radical displacement, thereby having
erupted as two large protuberances on the chest. More
surprisingly, the boy had smooth skin and was wearing
mascara! His pensive look seemed to reveal a tormented
soul, crying out over the current perverted state of the
society in which boys were slowly metamorphizing
into effeminate assortments. Meanwhile, Akbar came
to the main door and they walked in. Aziz Sahib's
pupils seemed to bounce in rhythm with the movement
of the newcomer's rump, till the time the door closed
behind them. Ali had left soon after.

* * *

There was commotion in the college library. Boys were
huddled around a table, looking intently at something.

Their excited voices seemed to be focused on some person they all knew. Ali stood on his toes and peered over them. He saw an open magazine, and a photograph being ogled at and discussed. He inquired about it from a boy standing closest to him.

The boy beamed, 'It is Asma. She has modelled for MAG. Boy, she is something to look at!'

Ali pushed his way through and took a closer look. Yes, it was Asma gracing the centrefold.

For the next three days, Akbar and Asma were nowhere to be found. Ali kept calling Akbar but there was no response. The operator at Akbar's house would not give him his whereabouts. The only piece of information he could wriggle out of him was that he was away from home and could not be reached. He tried to speak to his father's aide-de-camp, Wing Commander Jamal, with whom he had become good friends, but he too didn't answer his calls or call him back. And then, on the fourth day, Akbar called him in the afternoon.

'I cannot speak over the phone, come over now,' Akbar's voice sounded hollow.

The security guard at the entrance must have been new because he came up to the driver's side and asked Ali to roll down the window. Ali was in no mood to prove his credentials yet again to some idiot guarding the residence. Akbar's father had to be protected from the evils of the air and not the ground, he thought. There was a new guard team every time he visited.

Once again, he had to go through the security protocol before he was allowed to enter.

Thankfully he didn't have to wait long. As per the Standard Operating Procedure of the security manual, one had to take a right turn from the gate to reach the porch, although it was much shorter to go straight and then take a right. As one took a right turn, the vast lawn of the Air House came into view, culminating in a distant perimeter wall, neatly lined with poplars. The finely manicured lawn was relevant only on a few national days, when its fine blades were trampled under the boots of the mighty who ruled the land. Otherwise, for most of the year, it just lay there, waiting to be trodden upon. As they reached the porch, Aziz Sahib came running to take away his car to the parking.

The wall-to-wall carpeted hallway led to the drawing and dining rooms to the right and to a couple of guest rooms to the left. A large door at the end of the hallway opened to the residential quarters of Akbar's parents. The hallway took a sharp left, and at a short distance was Akbar's room. As he entered the room, the first thing he noticed was a new poster which was surely put up after his last visit: a young Caucasian girl with abundant hair, her greyish-blue eyes piercing through the poster into his own.

Ali was spellbound and couldn't take his eyes off her. Beauty is intimidating after all. *There was nothing better in the world than a Caucasian maiden,* he thought with a sigh. *Why couldn't God make such good-looking damsels in the East? Why test our faith all the time?* He had never seen this model before. It took him a while before he read her name at the bottom of the poster: Brooke Shields. While he was transfixed with her beauty, he did not realize that Amjad, the bearer, had entered the room and was asking him something. The spell was broken, and he realized Amjad was asking him to come with him to the back garden.

'You could have taken me directly there,' Ali told him.

'Sir, he thought he would meet you in his room but then he went out and now would like to see you there.'

Akbar was sitting on a swing in the back garden, using it like a rocking chair. It was late afternoon in March and the weather was pleasant. It didn't take long for Akbar to let Ali in on the latest developments.

The poplars were meant to block the intrusive rays of the sun, so as not to disturb the repose of the privileged inhabitants. Nevertheless, a couple of yellow streaks were able to breach the security, illuminating Akbar's forehead. He had to keep his head tilted in an awkward manner to avoid the rays falling directly into his eyes.

'But why Islamabad and at that time of the night? Do you realize who you are?' Ali's jaw dropped and his face became ridiculously distorted after listening to the story.

'Listen, Ali, I don't need a lecture on who I am.'

'Okay, but what made you take her to Islamabad at midnight?' Ali's arched eyebrows and his open mouth were begging for some plausible explanation.

Akbar looked up at Ali. His thick eyelashes behind his silver-rimmed glasses batted a few times.

'My mind was blocked. I had a very long argument with my mother. She came to know about the pictures. She even knew about her visits to the house. Aziz must have told her. But, anyway, she knew everything. She wanted me to leave her. I said no!'

There was a silence before Akbar continued, 'I guess I should have stopped at the checkpost. Asma got so scared. She couldn't stop screaming. They wouldn't believe who I was and hit me to get the truth. The day you brought the MAG, which had Asma's modelling pictures, I took them to show my mother as I wanted to take her into my confidence. When I entered her room, she had the same edition in her hands and was intently looking at her pictures. She never said anything; neither did I. Ali, let us go away for a few days to your village. What was the name? Yes, Charbagh. I want to get out of here for a few days. It will give me some time to think.'

A couple of days later, the entire school knew about the episode. The intrusive ones kept asking Ali what had happened; what their destination was; what were they doing when they were caught, etc. Ali just denied having any knowledge. They kept pestering him to tell them something, but he kept quiet. His demeanour only increased the distance between him and his classmates.

Asma could not face the sneer of her colleagues and decided to take leave. Girls had already started keeping their distance from her; after this episode they wouldn't even exchange greetings with her. Akbar told Ali that Asma's parents were angry with her. Her mother constantly blamed her husband for pampering her so much that she had brought dishonour to the family. With her movements restricted, Asma became a virtual prisoner in her own house.

With three months left for the final exams, it was a make-or-break situation for all students. Admission into professional universities was competitive, requiring an intensive study routine. Being pre-engineering students, both Akbar and Ali had to show a high level of commitment; distractions had to be kept to a minimum. In these final months, there was limited interaction between them. Even when they got together, conversation stayed within the confines of topics related to mathematics or physics.

After the exams, Akbar left for the US. The results were announced while he was there. He had managed to pass and was now busy with his admissions. Ali had also made the cut for the Engineering University in Peshawar. Asma had barely passed her premedical subjects and was not eligible for any professional university. The only way out for such students, besides a life of mourning, was to take arts or perhaps do a degree in management.

* * *

Ali met Asma at the college. Like all other students, she was there to clear her final dues at the accounts department. He was shocked to see that her hair was dishevelled. For the first time he saw her eyes listless and without mascara. She seemed to be in a hurry.

'How are you doing, Asma?'

'Yes good, I am fine,' she answered with a wry smile.

'What are your plans?'

'I await God's plan for me.' It was obvious to Ali that she was in a state of depression.

'I meant, have you decided which subjects you will take in the university?'

'I am still undecided,' Asma said and pouted to show helplessness.

'What about you?'

'Yes, I shall be joining the Engineering University in Peshawar. I am on the merit list.'

'Good for you, Ali. I knew you would make it.' Asma tried to smile.

'Shall we have a cup of tea at the cafeteria?'

'I have to rush. My mother needs the car.'

'Okay. Good to see you, Asma.'

'Yes, thanks Ali.'

During his conversation with the accountant, he came to know that Annie's father had been appointed principal of the college. This came as a surprise, since he was retired by now, and as far as he knew, the air force did not employ retired officers for these positions. As he was driving out of the parking lot of the college, he saw Annie get down from a blue Toyota Crown being driven by Aziz Sahib. He drove near the car and turned around to take a better look. Yes, it was Aziz Sahib.

It was after a break of six months that Akbar called Ali from Virginia. After the customary banter, Akbar told him that he was throwing a party on the first of January and that he must come.

'Why the first of January?'

'To have a great year ahead,' was Akbar's calm reply. 'Wear a suit, okay. One of your best ones,' Akbar directed him.

It was still early for other guests when Ali arrived. The Air House was lit up as he had never seen before. The first of January was not a national or religious day. He was escorted straight to Akbar's room. Akbar opened the door after a few knocks. His hair was neatly gelled, and he was immaculately dressed in a tuxedo.

'Hey, stranger! What is the occasion?' Ali asked excitedly.

'Well, it is my nikah.'

'Don't bullshit me.'

'No, no, I am serious. It is my nikah. Guests will soon start arriving.'

'I am glad for you and Asma.' Ali was excited for his best friend but then his expression changed. 'What does that look mean, Akbar?'

Akbar tilted his head and looked up at Ali, 'I am getting married to Annie.'

7

The Rebound

To Ali's surprise, the froth had moved to the bottom of the mug. He wasn't sure if the heat of Muscat had evaporated the coffee or if he had actually drunk it. If he had, then it must have taken him, given the size of the mug, at least half an hour. He looked at his watch; it was 5.30 p.m. There were two hours for the flight to land. He took a deep breath and looked around. The coffee shop was largely empty. In a corner, there was a young Omani boy earnestly vying to impress an older white lady. The boy, perhaps on a date with the first Caucasian he could get hold of—never mind her age—was talking enthusiastically, while the lady seemed to simper at his inexperience. Outside, under the green and yellow canopy, the al fresco sitting had attracted a couple of Omanis, who were acclimatized to the heat of Muscat.

As Ali's gaze swept across the place and settled on the crimson colour of the setting sun, it seemed to merge with the serene waters of the Gulf of Oman. He wondered why human beings were still fascinated by these mechanical processes of nature. But, today, his mind was quickly drawn from this repetitive calamity to the impending flight. He wasn't sure if he was taking the right step, and if so with what objective. For once, he wasn't sure about his own expectation. What would happen by the end of these two weeks? Was he alone in extending this hospitality or had he been subtly compelled to do it?

Life had been rewarding for Ali at every step. He had come a long way—from the corridors of PAF Degree College, Peshawar, to the auditoriums of the engineering and business universities and now the seaside coffee shop in Muscat. It had been seven years since he had left PAF Degree College. Since then, the pace of existence had snatched away the old friendships. He had hardly been in touch with anyone, and no one had made the effort to get in touch with him. He would often reminisce about his old friends, especially Akbar, but the modern societal expectation of being contacted first always became the barrier.

It had been almost a year since Ali's transfer to Muscat. It was a quiet town by Pakistani standards, located by the Red Sea, where people still found the time to balance business and pleasure. The lower number of inhabitants in contrast with the vast empty land offered greater possibilities of horizontal expansion. Ali strongly believed that the character of people changed once a city started expanding vertically. That is when the age-old traditions of hospitality and warmth got replaced without compunction. However, he was happy to be living here at a time when generosity and kindness were still prevalent.

After engineering, Ali had decided to switch his career to commerce, bidding goodbye to the horrors of mathematics. During all the years of studying the subject, he could never come to terms with the concept of deciphering nature with the science called mathematics. To him it was a distasteful exercise, carried out by a select few to claim superiority over others. How could nature fit into perfectly shaped triangles, squares and trapezoids? No wonder buildings collapsed, planes crashed and ships sank. Armed with this logic, it took him sixteen years before finally defenestrating this sign language and taking up commerce for a living. His first job was based in Islamabad, and within a few months he was asked to move to Muscat with the same bank.

For the first time in his life, Ali realized the importance of coffee shops. These watering holes were a boon for lonely expatriates. After trying out several, he had finally settled for D'Arcy's Kitchen as his favourite place. The vibrant green and yellow colours, the comprehensive menu and the availability of all the dishes on a regular basis, had hooked him on to this coffee shop. But life was still lonely, and he tried to cross the short distance to Pakistan as frequently as he could.

It had been a pleasant surprise when Ali had seen Asma standing at the counter, holding a prescription, trying to decipher a doctor's handwriting. He was visiting Peshawar after almost seven years. The customer was of little help, as both tried to reach some definitive conclusion. He had never seen her in the store before: it was her father who ran the pharmacy. As he came closer to the counter, she looked up at him, held her breath for a split second before crying out, 'Return of the stranger.' Her eyes became ebullient as she extended her hand to Ali. The customers were visibly shocked to see this public display of affection in Peshawar.

Asma was so happy to see Ali that she asked him to accompany her home for a more detailed chat. Both were eager to catch up on the events of the past seven years. They settled down in Asma's lounge before she started narrating her story. In the dark he could faintly make out the furnishings of the snug little lounge. She told him that her parents had passed away and her only surviving brother was in the US. Her current struggle was trying to manage her father's pharmaceutical business. As her sombre voice flowed through the dark, the lamp on the side table projected her larger-than-life predicament on the opposite wall in the form of her own shadow. The power system was out of order and load-shedding was at its peak.

Asma described her disappointment when Akbar told her on the phone that he was under immense pressure from his family. She knew all along that his mother was against the match and would go to any lengths to convince her son against the arrangement; but she had not imagined that he would give up so easily. The engagement had taken place just to pour water over the fire. His father, who until then had supported Akbar, also took a firm stand against their marriage. She was devastated: Akbar was the love of her life. After his marriage, she closeted herself in the house. Her school and college mates could not risk associating themselves with her. After all, they aspired to have lasting marriages. And then a distant cousin of hers—a decade older—asked for her hand in marriage. The nikah was solemnized, and she was sent packing to Lahore. No one had cared to ask her; enough dishonour had been heaped upon the family.

She just couldn't accept him as her husband. She would wince every time he would try to get close to her; she just couldn't get over Akbar. Initially he was patient and gave her time to come to terms with her changed circumstances, but after about a year of rejection, he exploded. He beat her up repeatedly. How could the marriage continue? She looked up at Ali wryly. 'We got divorced a little after one year.'

'What about your parents?' asked Ali in a voice full of apprehension.

'My parents! Yes, my mother passed away soon after Akbar got married; my father, a year ago. Both my elder brothers died as well.'

Four people from the same family passing in a span of seven years seemed stranger than fiction. It was as if they had planned it. So, she was on her own now, all by herself in this male-dominated city of Peshawar.

'Ali, I know we didn't spend much time together in the college, but you are my only connection with the past.' Her rheumy eyes filled up with tears. She tied her hair in a bun and looked up at him after narrating her ordeal. The expectant look in those dark eyes was spellbinding.

During the entire monologue, except for getting a clarification here or there, Ali had not uttered a single coherent sentence. He just did not know what to say or how to comfort her. The Panglossian maxim, 'everything is for the best', didn't fit here; he tried hard to slip in some religious platitude to console her, but couldn't find an opportune one that would compensate for the loss of four family members. With his eyes fixed on the carpet, he just kept uttering the familiar sounds affirming his attentiveness as Asma enumerated one misfortune after the other.

'What about you? You haven't said a word.'

Ali didn't have a story. As he began his seven-year narrative, he realized that the years had passed without any undue interference from nature. He felt ashamed to say that his parents were still alive and that everything was smooth. Life had not chosen him for any dramatic upheaval until then, and on his part, he was too risk-averse to create one for himself. The pattern drawn out for him by his parents didn't leave any place for distraction. Wading through life was a serious affair which had to be carried out with one's head high above water. One slip and there was no guarantee of emerging ever again. He had led a regimented life with this conviction, fully immersed in books to avoid any unexpected dunks. Now, overwhelmed by her story, he didn't have any other choice but to leave. He had no words to console her. So, despite her pleas, he told her that his flight to Muscat was booked from Lahore, and prior to the flight he had to meet someone. Realizing that it was a long drive from Peshawar to Lahore, Asma reluctantly agreed.

* * *

The flight was booked for midnight. The atmosphere on the rooftop restaurant was festive. As Ali looked towards the ancient mosque, he noticed that the minarets were illuminated by spotlights placed at the bottom, while the main mosque and its large courtyard lay in gloom: the wilful blackness intentionally left to faith for illumination. For thousands of years, man had endeavoured to leave a permanent imprint on the earth's wide canvas, where he liberally demonstrated his fears, his hopes, his aspirations and his loss for the world to appreciate. The current admirers of the visible enterprise, the Badshahi Mosque, constituted diners only. 'Are you here, Ali?' Aqsa's mildly irritated voice shook him out of his reverie.

'Yes. I was just thinking . . . actually I wasn't thinking. I was just looking at the mosque.'

'What about it? You have been here so many times.'

Ali and Aqsa had been engaged for almost two years. Aqsa had painstakingly managed this rendezvous after a lot of tactical manoeuvring. Her father had dropped her off at her cousin's, and here she was with her fiancé. Her father, an ex-army man, had obstinately stuck to his ways, rarely allowing his daughter to go anywhere unless accompanied by her mother. The army and his conservative sense of honour never left him, and he ran the family like a regiment. Feeling emancipated for once, despite the fact that she was engaged, Aqsa's halal adventure was being ruined by Ali's distracted state of mind.

* * *

Over the next three months, Ali and Asma regularly spoke over the telephone on weekends, talking for hours on end. Asma always had so much to talk about, and Ali seemed addicted to her soft voice. He confided to her that he had never spoken with anyone for so long and on such a regular basis.

'No, not even Aqsa,' he told her. 'I don't know how to explain it to you.' Asma could feel him struggling to find the right words.

'I will be visiting soon; try to explain it in words.'

The next weekend, Ali was in Islamabad on the pretext of visiting his parents.

* * *

'Could you just slow down,' Asma bent down holding her sides and panting heavily.

'Well, it was you who tried to intimidate me with your ladies' gym routine in Peshawar,' Ali let out a chuckle.

'Can we rest for a moment?' As Asma balanced herself on a rock, she couldn't help appreciating the view.

'It is a beautiful sight. One can see half of Islamabad from here,' Asma remarked as she tried to catch her breath.

'There was a time when you could see the entire city from this spot.'

'Why, what happened? Did the mountain shrink?'

Ali laughed heartily.

'So, what are your plans? When are you leaving for Muscat?'

'Day after tomorrow. And when are you planning to visit me?'

'What for?' The glint in her eyes clearly showed her affectionate frivolity.

'Sorry I asked.'

Asma let out a hearty laugh, got up and put her arm around Ali.

'Grumpy old man!'

'Come on, we still have some way to go before we reach that stupid vantage point of yours.' Asma got up from the boulder she was sitting on and starting walking.

As Ali followed her, he could not help but say, 'Only if you have good eyesight to appreciate the view from that point. Should have worn your glasses today.' Asma made a face as Ali smiled.

* * *

He was at the office when he received a call from his mother. Though he had a cell phone, his mother usually called him on his landline during office hours. She sounded upset. Aqsa's parents had been asking them about the marriage date. They wanted them to get married before he left for Muscat, but Ali had flatly refused, citing career as a priority at that stage in his life. In the various conversations with Aqsa on the phone he would repeat the same argument.

'How can I give you any comfort when I am not even settled yet?'

'But I want us to be together. I will never ask for anything,' Aqsa would reply innocently.

During those telephone calls, Ali would imagine Aqsa's expression. He would imagine her innocent face embellished by frizzy golden-brown hair, looking up to him questioningly. She had a delicate nose and an attractive mouth, but it was her smile that he found disarming. She had a classical upbringing: English education at a convent, a bachelor's degree from a decent college, and now, like any other girl of her age, looking forward to a lifetime of marriage. Genetically programmed, she saw marriage as the culmination of her career.

Ali's mother wanted the arrangement to be formalized at the earliest. 'Long engagements are disastrous,' she would say. In his one year at Muscat, this was the third call he had received from her regarding the subject. In fact, his mother had been pestering him since he was in the last quarter of his MBA programme. But he had wanted to settle down before taking on the burden of marriage. The expression, 'to settle down', among the many borrowed from the West, was used to enjoy the pleasures of life before getting into an insipid marriage. Meanwhile, parents looked forward to getting their children married as soon as their education was over. They believed procreation to be the right diversion for any right-thinking graduate. Any delays, as per their logic, could result in discontinuation of the human race. But things were slowly beginning to change. Boys and girls from good families—euphemistically representing the aristocracy—were taking their time when it came to tying the knot. They believed in knowing their partner well before accepting a lifetime of commitment. Larger number of women were entering universities every year and ending up in the corporate world. As a result, their new-found emancipation was bringing about changes in the social structure as well. The timid caricature of a dependent housewife was slowly giving way to a confident working woman equally supporting the household.

The new generation was more inward-looking; hooked to the pursuit of self-gratification. Instead of being concerned with the institution of marriage as an objective in itself, these youngsters felt perturbed with the limited possibilities of pleasure in a rigid shell of social conformity. They couldn't imagine spending an entire lifetime with a single person.

So, when Ali's mother, through her Charbagh connection, had the perfect match for him, he had resisted the idea. But the rigidity of Charbagh's blood had eventually prevailed. She was the eldest daughter of Khan Sahib, married to a bureaucrat, and so her vision for her family was engraved in stone. She had played her cards so well that Ali was forced to yield to her choice. His father, a man of few words, had kept his distance, nodding to the idea when required to do so. But now he wanted some time to himself. Ever since he had met Asma after a seven-year break, he felt it was his duty to comfort her.

* * *

Asma was pleasantly surprised when she reached Muscat. While she was expecting it to be a one-horse town, the city had all the amenities any First World country could offer. Even the airport was better developed than the ones at Peshawar and Islamabad. And on his part, Ali had laid down an itinerary for her visit. In fact, Asma found it funny when on her way to Ali's flat he handed over a two-week stay plan, complete with sites, dates and time. Having taken days off, Ali intended to show the best of Muscat and the surrounding areas to Asma.

After having exhausted the cultural, historical and shopping sites, day seven was reserved for the beach. 'Are you serious? I have been given a visitor visa as your sister?' Asma couldn't believe it when Ali told her that. 'And you are telling me this after a whole week!'

Asma had stopped in her tracks, and, instead of looking at the beautiful sunset on the pristine beach near D'Arcy's, was staring at Ali with a look that was somewhere between incredulity and amusement. But she soon gathered herself and with a mischievous smile retorted, 'Yes, why not. Let us be siblings. It will make life so much easier.' The golden rays of the sun seemed to set her face ablaze as she squinted her eyes at him. Ali smiled at her amusing reaction.

'Why don't you take off your shoes?' she suddenly asked him. 'Feel the cool sand against your feet. It is so therapeutic.'

'No, it is okay. I like it this way.'

'Why are you so uptight, Ali? Relax. I never realized Muscat would be so restorative in mind and body. See, close your eyes and breathe deeply. Let your stale banking air out and fresh air in.'

Asma closed her eyes, lifted her arms and took deep breaths. As Ali stared at her affectionately, the sound of the waves breaking on the shore provided the perfect background music to a new story taking shape.

* * *

Like all desert towns, Muscat shook off its slumber in the evening as well. That was the time when the town seemed to be reborn. People thronged to the restaurants and bars. It was dinner time, and Ali had brought Asma to the best restaurant in town at the Al Bustan Palace hotel. Initially meant to be a palace, His Majesty, the sultan of Oman, had graciously opened it to the public. Built on the shores of the Red Sea, this white gem rose majestically against serrated black hills. For a first-time visitor, the immense size of the hotel atrium, elaborately decorated with the choicest marble, was awe-inspiring.

The hotel was a maze of galleries, rooms and halls. It took them a while to find their way to the restaurant. The singer at the restaurant had been especially flown in from Lebanon. She was heavily decked up and was wearing a red dress that amply showed her cleavage. She moved from one table to the other, asking the diners to dance with her. Asma didn't require any urging when the singer approached her and held her hand to make her dance. To everyone's pleasant surprise, Asma's sensual movements were so appropriate to the song that the audience could not help clapping for her. Not only that but she also lip-synced the song. The Lebanese singer hugged her, and Asma sat back smiling.

'What was that? How did you know the song?' Ali was surprised.

'It is the latest from this Egyptian singer, Amr Diab; pretty famous in the Arab world.'

'Wow! But you never told me you could dance.'

'Well, it takes time to discover these things.' Asma flicked back her hair and preened herself in front of Ali.

Asma had spent almost ten days in Muscat and the difference in their relationship was visible. For the entire first week, their conversations had centred on Akbar. Her visit was immersed in nostalgia, as if asking Ali to move back the clock and play an active role in rearranging her past. She told Ali that after her break-up with Akbar, her efforts to fill her emptiness with God and business both ended in failure. She sold her business and told God to be patient with her until she went back to praising Him. 'After all, He had time written on His hands, I didn't,' she said. And here she was in Muscat, reconnecting with her past, hoping to alter it somehow.

Asma was not happy with Ali's choice of interiors and had rearranged his one-bedroom apartment. They had gone out and bought a couple of rugs for the sitting area, and the sofa was replaced with a larger, colourful one. The new arrangement suited the open-kitchen layout of the chic flat. The limited space was amply compensated by the view of the Red Sea. These were the perks of being in the corporate world.

From day one, Ali had insisted that Asma sleep in the bedroom and he in the lounge. But she would always reject the idea forcefully.

'No. I will sleep in the lounge. I will be more comfortable on the sofa.'

'A locked bedroom will ensure the avoiding of deviant urges,' Ali would say with a mischievous smile on his face.

'I can rein in my urges and can discipline yours. I don't need a locked bedroom for that,' she would retort, squinting her eyes and pursing her lips before flashing her signature smile. It was this smile that had melted the hearts of many during her college days.

From the first day of her stay in Muscat, Asma had insisted on making breakfast. Every morning when Ali stepped into the lounge, Asma would be sitting there, watching TV or reading a magazine. She would ask him to sit on the sofa and get busy in the kitchen, preparing breakfast for him. He would feel embarrassed but couldn't match her obstinacy. She didn't want to be reminded that she was a guest.

One evening, both decided to stay back and watch TV together. Staring blankly into the television screen, they involuntarily held each other's hand. Taking further initiative, Asma took Ali's hand and put it in her lap, tightly clasping it between hers.

'Why can't we be together, Asma?'

There was a long pause before Asma answered, 'I don't want to be another Annie.'

What followed was a long conversation. Asma was apprehensive. Her comment that she didn't want to be another Annie should have sealed the matter. But Ali wanted clarity. Men are so strange; there is nothing subtle about them and their dealings. They want to hear what they want to hear and in so many words.

Ali thought he could jolt Asma by asking her, 'So, why are you here in Muscat with me?'

Instead, Asma looked up at him calmly and said, 'I have told you. You are my only connection with the past. You somehow preserve the moments that I have always cherished.'

Once again, the spectre of Akbar had been resurrected. He let go of Asma's hand and tried to get up, only to be restrained by her.

'Wait, look at me.' The determined look in her dark eyes forced him to sit back.

'I do not want anyone to suffer because of me.'

Ali kept quiet. Asma retook Ali's hand and clasped it even more tightly.

Asma broke the silence. 'Akbar tried to contact me a couple of months ago.'

'Why? Isn't he happily married to his muse?' The surprise in Ali's voice was audible.

'Annie and Akbar broke up. She is back in Pakistan. They didn't have any children.'

'What does he want now? Why is he calling you? And, more importantly, what do you want?'

'How can I trust him again?' Asma seemed to go into deep contemplation.

'Why are you telling me this?' Asma could sense Ali's irritation.

'Just like that. Maybe you would like to contact him?'

'After what he did to you?'

To defuse the tension, Asma asked Ali to go for a walk. He was stubbornly resistant and literally had to be pulled out of the sofa. There was a walking trail just behind Ali's building. Evenings were always pleasant, and the light breeze at the time made the atmosphere even more vibrant. There were spots along the path where there was thick vegetation, making one feel safe from prying eyes. For a long time, Ali had fantasized about falling in love at that spot. And now that he was there with Asma, he could realize his fantasy. But not in his current mental state, when he felt so emotionally drained. Once again it was Asma who took the lead. She stopped at the same spot and turned towards him. She looked into his eyes and pulled him towards her, hugging him tightly. That night, Asma didn't need much persuasion to sleep in the bedroom.

* * *

All good things come to an end. Asma left a couple of days later. Ali felt lonely and miserable. This was the first weekend since her departure. He sat in the lounge, savouring the moments they had spent together. The half-empty sofa stared at him. Just when he was relishing the most intimate moment with Asma, his cell phone buzzed. He didn't recognize the number; it was from Pakistan. He reluctantly answered the phone and said hello in an unfriendly voice, only to realize it was Akbar.

He didn't know how to react. Akbar was visiting his parents in Islamabad after a long time and had taken his number from his mother. As expected, Ali's mother had given him all the current details. Ali was abrupt with him when it came to Asma, berating him for not standing by her. All Akbar could mutter was, 'Yes, but I will make it up to her.'

'And how do you plan to do that?' was Ali's irritable reply to Akbar's calm pronouncement. As Ali became more irritated, Akbar begged leave, promising to call him some other time.

The next day, Ali's mother called. She was very upset. She knew about Asma's visit and that she had stayed with him in Muscat. Who could have told her, he wondered. Yes, Asma had met her a couple of times and had her contact but couldn't be the one giving herself away. And then she dropped a bombshell: 'Listen, I cannot risk my reputation and that of our family by letting you besmirch our name. If you don't feel settled now, you will never be in a hundred years. I cannot play with the life of an innocent girl. This is an honourable family we are dealing with. You do whatever you feel like. I am cancelling your engagement!' And she banged down the phone. Landline phones provided her the flexibility of utilizing her ego to its fullest when required. Mobile phones were not cut out for the task.

In his desperation, Ali tried calling Asma, but she didn't reply. He had bought her a cell phone in Muscat and had spoken to her a couple of times. Texting had not evolved yet, so people still spoke to each other. Both of them had worked out their future plans—he had to deal with his engagement, and she had to take care of her property in Peshawar. Once these issues were out of the way, she would move to Muscat with him. And before that he would visit Pakistan and convince his parents about the change in his marriage plans. It was simple. He was getting married as required but to a different girl. The important thing was his belief in the institution of marriage; the choice of partner was secondary.

* * *

It was a painful one week before he received a call from Asma. She asked him to listen to her calmly and not interrupt. Asma brought up the topic of his engagement and repeated that she did not want to destroy anyone's family. Hearing the same issues again, Ali started to get worked up. He tried to convince her not to go back on their mutually agreed plan. As the conversation became animated, Asma cut the line. He tried calling her back several times, but she had switched off the phone.

For the first time in his life, an unplanned situation stared Ali in the face. The unedited script of life mocked him. In the coming days, he tried calling Asma many times, but her phone was perpetually turned off. He desperately needed someone to comfort him but couldn't find anyone. After a week, he received a call from his mother. As firm as always, she didn't have much time for pleasantries.

'I have safely managed to break up your engagement. Had it not been for me, these people would have lynched you for the dishonour you brought upon them. I told them that the company did not provide accommodation in the first two years of service. And they were not willing to have Aqsa married and live separately from you for so long.'

'And one more thing before I hang up,' his mother's voice changed dramatically. 'That stupid girl, what was her name, yes, Asma, the one you entertained in Muscat. Do you know what she has done? She has gone off to the US with Akbar.'

8

The Office

The bank's head office building stood quietly by the main road, pondering its impact over the city. It was bathed in golden light, and the azure sky dotted with wisps of white provided it the perfect backdrop. It radiated prosperity. Its facade, with imposing pillars, exuded grandeur. The large glass panels allowed outsiders a sneak view of the corporate enterprise. The privileged inhabitants of the building had an unobstructed view of the expansive golf course just beyond the road. It was difficult to distinguish between the animated and the inanimate parts of the building. Its occupants sat fastened to their chairs, becoming part of the architecture. Prior to getting hypnotized by the radiance of its golden light, these automatons were still alive. But after having entered the building, the halo of prosperity had extinguished their individuality. Nevertheless, beneath the soothing

136

calm of the building lay the unseen turbulence of the corporate world.

It was 7.30 p.m., and the long summer day was coming to an end. Inside the building, some workstations were still lit. On the third floor, in a dimly lit cubicle, a weary-looking Imran took a deep breath and sat back in his chair. As he looked around, he realized his colleagues had left. Office timings were till 5.30 p.m. and most of them usually left by 6 p.m. But the nature of the work he handled almost always kept him in the office till 9 p.m. He took a quick glance at the clock on the taskbar of his laptop. Dinner was scheduled at 8 p.m., and it usually took him half an hour to reach home. He had promised himself that he would not miss this important family event at his parents'. All his brothers and sisters were to be there. But given the impending deadline, he wasn't sure if he could make it on time.

It was not the first time he had faced this dilemma; by now he had become used to it. Everyone was born with a purpose: he was meant to create spreadsheets. The file in front of him carried thousands of cells awaiting his command to reach their maximum potential. The satisfaction of observing thousands of values change in the spreadsheet by changing the value in one key cell was enormous. It took years to master such proficiency. But it came with a price. Imran could not remember attending any family function, be it a wedding or a funeral, in years. He would promise his family that he would spend time with them on weekends, only to find some urgent project that gobbled up his plans. He couldn't remember spending an entire fun-filled day with them.

Both his children, a girl and a boy of seven and five, were becoming used to life without him. They had stopped waiting for him. Even on weekends, they never asked him to take them out, knowing he would be tired as always. He distinctly remembered one night, when his daughter woke up in the dead of the night, came over to his side of the bed, kissed him and left the room. He could never get it out of his mind, cherishing the moment. As he remembered it now, tears came to his eyes.

His son had called him many times during office hours, only to hear his father ask him to hang up because he was busy. He didn't have the luxury of time to hear his son talk about the relevance of dinosaurs in human life. After a few unsuccessful attempts, he had given up and never called again. What did he really expect from his son: To give him an update on the economy or some inside information on a company that was on the brink of collapse? But he sincerely believed he was not to be blamed. These were the demands of a corporate life. He was a busy man and felt good about it. There was a lot of satisfaction in the claim of being busy. It showed his competence and professionalism. But as he started gaining the respect of his peers and seniors, it extracted a cost.

He was brusque with his wife, blaming her for not being able to understand the intricacies of corporate life. And he would laugh off his parents' apprehensions about his health. After all, he was the product of the new generation, fully aware of the requirements of life. But as he delved deeper into the cells of the spreadsheets, he got lost, unable to find his way out. The program had a unique quality: it let you enter but didn't let you leave. He was addicted to the sound of his keyboard. The clicking carried a symphony of its own, covering everything with the unseen layers of sound. It was a matter of time before someone would find a way of peeling them off from the various objects, converting them into formidable pieces of orchestra. Only then would people be able to see the pain and suffering behind those clicks. Nevertheless, Imran felt in charge of his life only when he worked on his laptop. He felt as if each cell looked up to him in veneration, eagerly waiting to carry out his command.

Imran shook his head and got back to work. After working for another half an hour according to his estimation, he looked at the clock. It was 9.30 p.m. He looked at his cell phone to reconfirm. Yes, it was 9.30 p.m.

* * *

Shehryar didn't seem too impressed by the report. He had asked Imran to provide him a detailed sensitivity analysis. What Imran had provided was factual performance only.

As Imran tried to explain, he was cut short by Shehryar.

'Imran, I have a meeting with the president in half an hour. What do you expect me to tell him?'

Imran had put in a lot of hard work and was expecting, if not appreciation, then a word of encouragement. He had been sitting late consistently for days to complete this project, ignoring his chronic sinus. This was not the first time he had ignored his recurring physical ailment for work. He was obsessed and wanted to impress his boss.

Phlegmatic to the extent of being depressed, Shehryar was fastidious as well. A short man, he was as complex as his curly hair. He was judgemental to the extent of being captious and had the talent of bringing out the worst in people. He could find fault with almost everything presented to him, without the ability to explain how to get it right. What the staff dreaded was the so-called interaction with them post his scrutiny. During these unending sessions, Shehryar would drone on about the work he had to handle because of his staff's oversight. He would get easily irritated with explanations and was convinced of the irrefutability of his point of view. A single sentence in one's defence meant an hour of torturous droning. The staff, therefore, preferred to keep quiet. Imran tried to wriggle out of this session by promising to do better but wasn't let off so easily. During the hour-long interaction, Shehryar repeated the same thing fifteen times, lecturing him on how to interpret his instructions more effectively. Unfortunately, Shehryar's tirades were of no consequence. His instructions would change at whim, confusing the staff. The only real impact it made was making everyone feel worthless. The staff was so scared and demotivated that they were always on the lookout for other, more suitable, jobs.

It was rumoured that in his previous job, an analyst, after being subjected to rigorous criticism over a long period, had finally lost his patience and slapped Shehryar. As expected, he was promptly dismissed from service. The onlookers described the expression of pride he carried when he was being led out of the office by the security.

Imran was a simple person, perhaps too simple to understand Shehryar's machinations. He kept trying to come up to his expectations, but in vain. He was supposed to be the best at his work, but he was often made to realize his managerial shortcomings. The spreadsheets were his forte, but he was told that if he wanted to get ahead in life, he needed to improve his managerial skills. Till he did that, he could not expect to get a promotion.

In the corporate world, men and women were meant to be managed in large cells called offices. It was here that their dark sides were chiselled and nurtured. Unfortunately for Imran, he had managed only the cells in spreadsheets. He did not realize that to survive and progress in the corporate world, one had to wear a thick layer of callousness, within which the corporate system artfully sowed seeds of greed, commonly called progress. He did not realize that it was greed that animated the earth in general and corporates in particular. After all, how could progress be achieved without greed? How could corporates bring out the best in their workers without invoking envy? Without wrath, how could the sloth be handled? And with progress came confidence, called pride.

What good had humility offered to mankind except meekness? Though Imran knew the virtues of evil, his malevolent barometer required a major shake-up. Fully aware that he had only a single lifetime, he still experimented with patience, abstinence, morality, honour and decency.

Farid, Saleem Khan's eldest son and a colleague of Imran, tried to snap him out of his goodness. He held long sessions with Imran, asking him to try and adopt at least some of the time-tested variables for success. Although a couple of years junior to Imran, Farid had promptly understood the requirements of life at an early age. Despite that, he genuinely cared about Imran. He squirmed with anger when Shehryar berated Imran over trivial matters without caring that he was doing so publicly. In one of the meetings, Shehryar had pushed Imran to the limit, without ascertaining if it was his fault in the first place. Imran had later told Farid, 'I couldn't sleep the entire night thinking what would I do if I lost this job?'

Farid always wondered what he would do if Shehryar behaved with him the way he did with Imran. His blood would boil, and he would be reminded of Lala's son, Ataullah, the warrior figure of his village. He knew that Ataullah was just a call away and would do anything for him. After all, Saleem Khan's eldest son, the future Khan of Charbagh, could not be insulted. Farid was furious with Imran for not defending himself and would call him a doormat. But Imran would just smile wryly and dismiss it as a corporate aberration.

Farid couldn't stand Shehryar any more and was fortunate to find another job. To honour a good friend and colleague, Imran arranged a send-off for him. At that time, Imran did not realize that this send-off would become such an issue.

'How could you arrange a send-off for him?' Shehryar was furious. 'He always worked against the interest of our group, and you gave him a send-off? You should have checked with me first.'

'Sir, you were on a visit, and we thought it would be a good idea to honour a colleague.'

Imran stroked his hair as if trying to stop a body blow with his hand.

'Why did you take such a big decision on your own? You should have waited for me to return.'

'Sir, we were hardly ten people, and it took fifteen minutes.'

'It is not about the time or the number of people. It is about principle. How can a person with an attitude be given a send-off?'

After half an hour of unnecessary tirade, Imran left the room with a limping ego. He felt like breaking the glass on his door but was too scared to jeopardize his career.

This was not the first time Shehryar had berated him, but this episode had left Imran seething with anger. After having given his best for the past four years, all he had received was undue censure. He had been intimidated for too long and was now fed up of living a life of fear. There were times when he would get up in the middle of the night, sweating and palpitating. The cardiac specialists he consulted gave him a clean chit but with a warning to give up smoking and reduce work-related stress. Otherwise, the doctor told him clearly, it could have serious implications. The prognosis had left him even more scared.

* * *

Shehryar had long cherished the dream of becoming the president of the bank. To achieve his objective, he was willing to slaughter anything that came in his way. The first thing he sacrificed was humility. He sincerely believed in humility being the enemy of success: to become a president, one needed the right demeanour for the job. So, he successfully threw out all forms of modesty from his system and created an impervious facade of sombreness. The only people who saw him smile were the president or members of the board of directors. His staff believed his mouth was not created to smile. So when he did try the inevitable in forced circumstances, his smile would constitute a painful stretching of the mouth, giving the impression of facial paralysis.

Imran was one of those people who had given up all his interests for the sake of his career. There was a time when he liked playing the harmonium. On one occasion, when he was asked to play at a corporate dinner, Shehryar had strongly objected. He was told that the fact that he was promoting himself through means other than work was not appreciated. He was no longer interested in watching cricket as well. He distinctly remembered the dates when he had to smother his desire to watch a cricket match and instead sit in front of his laptop to complete an assignment. He worked hard on weekdays and spent his weekends worrying over losing his job. Even the time he spent outside the office made him anxious and he yearned to go back to his seat to see the flicker of the screen and hear the sound of the keyboard. Otherwise, how would he feed his family?

Imran had the choice of walking out of the organization, away from Shehryar. But meeting another potential employer was risky. If someone snitched on him and the other company did not make a final offer, he could lose his current job. What would he do then? Where would he go? Who would support his wife and children? His parents already lived with his brothers, ruling out any possibility of moving in with them.

It was in these moments of melancholy that he called Farid and requested him to arrange for a Zigana, a semi-automatic Turkish pistol that he had seen with him. Farid was brought up in an environment where guns were worshipped. He often spoke to Imran about his formidable collection. Intrigued by his claims, Imran had visited Farid's house to confirm this. For a person who had never held a gun in his hand, the collection seemed impressive. Out of the collection, this pistol had left a mark on Imran's mind. So, it came as a huge surprise to Farid when a person as submissive as Imran requested him to buy him a gun and arrange for a licence as well. He became suspicious. A gun in the hands of a novice posed greater danger as compared to someone trained in its handling. To carry a gun required years of discipline. When Farid probed Imran on why he suddenly needed a gun, he obliquely mentioned the deteriorating law-and-order situation of the city. Farid wasn't convinced but couldn't say no to Imran. In less than a month, an all-Pakistan licence was arranged, and the gun along with a box containing a hundred bullets was delivered at Imran's residence. Farid couldn't resist advising him, 'Never point it at anyone, even in jest. This is the basic discipline of owning a gun. And do not carry it with you. Just keep it handy on your bedside table for intruders.'

The black and grey gun was such a visual delight: Imran would keep stroking it gently until someone would interrupt, breaking the spell. Whenever he was alone in a room, he would play with it. He felt the same excitement he once felt while watching cricket or playing the harmonium. He would take the pistol out of its black box and keep aiming it in different directions. After a long time, Imran had found delight in an object outside the cells of a spreadsheet.

* * *

Meanwhile, in the office, a presentation to the board of directors was planned. The chairman of the board wanted a detailed analysis of industry trends and the bank's response. The president asked Shehryar to present it on behalf of the bank. This was a God-given opportunity for Shehryar to have his credentials stamped by the board. If he could impress the members, no one could jeopardize his position as the next president.

It was a nightmare for Imran: the presentation had to be delivered without compromising the overwhelming daily work. For an entire week he forgot that he had a family or a life of his own. But as luck would have it, just two days before the presentation, Imran's daughter fell sick with pneumonia. His wife, with the help of his brother, arranged her admission into a hospital. It was only on the third day, on the eve of the presentation, that Imran visited his daughter.

'Baba, you were busy in the office? I told mama not to call you.'

Not knowing what to say, Imran started sobbing like a child. His wife and children were surprised to see him cry. Men were not supposed to show their emotions. It was shocking for them to see the cover of his resolute self blown away by sentiment. He cried for a long time. When he couldn't stop despite his best efforts, his brother had to help him leave the room.

The next day, Shehryar called Imran. He was shaking with anger. 'How could you leave when we had to do a final revision of the presentation?'

After hearing Imran's explanation, all Shehryar said was, 'We all have family issues. Don't you know my father is on a ventilator? But does it stop me from carrying out my duties?'

The presentation was very well-received by the board members. However, Shehryar pointed out to Imran that in one place he had forgotten to specifically mention if the figures were in billions or trillions of rupees, causing him huge embarrassment. *This was the best I could have done*, thought Imran. Without asking for permission, he gave his boss a wry smile and left the room. He couldn't get his daughter's sick face out of his mind. Her words kept haunting him for days. He was still seething with anger and tried to find a target to let off steam. Though he couldn't find one, he got scared of himself: he had never had such a rush of blood before.

* * *

It was just a matter of one month. Shehryar's candidature as president had been finalized, and his dream of occupying the most lucrative seat was finally becoming a reality. He must have smiled on the occasion, but no one ever got to see it.

With Shehryar's departure, Imran found some respite. Even while he was his boss, Imran had identified a position in another department but was scared to ask him. Now Imran could request him for the promotion. Given the protocol, Imran had to take an appointment with him through his secretary. In the past two weeks, Imran had asked Susan at least four times, but there had been no response. On one occasion, Imran saw Shehryar on his floor and went up to him to make the request. As Imran walked up to him with a broad smile, a cold stare greeted him. Shehryar politely told him to meet him some other time as he was very busy. This was a typical Shehryar shtick: making the other person feel unwanted. Deeply angered, Imran pondered the alacrity with which he would jump to Shehryar's call at inconvenient times. He tried meeting him one last time. Susan was abrupt and her tone was derogatory.

'Look, Imran, I have asked the president many times. This time when I asked, he told me to tell you to meet your new boss and stop bothering him. Now you tell me what should I do?'

Imran spent that evening locked up in his study, staring at his Zigana, the new-found Turkish love of his life. The next day, Imran went late to the office. Without going to his cubicle, he took the executive glass lift. As the lift ascended towards the executive floor, he saw some golfers and felt envious. He couldn't believe people could indulge in leisure on a working day, without worrying about sustenance. How he wished he were one of them. The words of his parents resounded in his mind, 'There is life outside your office as well.' As he reached the executive floor, instead of walking straight into the president's office, he walked out towards the terrace and stood staring at the traffic on the main road. He saw a beeline of cars, vans, rickshaws and motorcycles moving in both directions. These were the cells of life, moving about without the click of a button. They just kept moving devoid of any rhythm, producing the ugliest of sounds. He noticed the trees that looked bored in their brown trunks and wondered what value they added to a centrally air-conditioned office. He looked up at the blue sky and felt smothered by the limitation it offered.

Susan saw Imran and wondered what he was doing on the terrace. No one ever dared go up to the terrace of the executive floor, standing, looking out at the passing traffic. Professionals did not indulge in such cameos. She realized he was wearing a suit for a change, instead of his signature checked shirt and trousers. After what must have been half an hour, she saw him leave the terrace and walk towards her. As he came closer, she saw an elegantly dressed but a sombre-looking Imran. His unkempt hair seemed to be forced into compliance through generous use of gel. To her surprise, the submissiveness was gone, and he walked in with confidence. He saw through her when she looked up at him expectantly. He walked past her and before she realized it, he had entered the president's room. She rushed to stop him but by that time he was already inside. Unable to stop him at the right moment, she thought it prudent to retreat to her seat. She had barely settled down when she jumped at the sound of two shots fired in quick succession inside the president's room.

As Shehryar sat cowering in his chair, staring at the bullet mark on his table, the security personnel were busy removing Imran's bloodied body from his office. He had shot himself in the head.

9

The Revenge

A polo-neck jumper is not a garment; it is a fashion statement for people endowed with long necks. Whether it is the clasping version, wound tightly around the neck or a baggy version, one requires the right anatomy to pull it off. Shazia preferred the latter. While talking, she would hold the neckband, displaying her soft skin, and while listening, she liked covering her hands in the long sleeves by tugging at the cuff. It was enticing to see her white hands emerge from the safety of the wool into the treacherous world of profit and loss.

In office, her long fingers did not hesitate to punch the keyboard with force, skilfully saving the manicured nails from damage. Shazia represented the new crop of deviant youth, intent on reaping the benefits of progress without compromising on their freedom. Her closest friends were married off, but, for her, finding a permanent headache was not a priority. She was part of an enviable group that led a life of emancipation. She looked forward to reaching somewhere in her banking career before contemplating if the planet still required her indomitable genes. Reaching somewhere was the predicament of the new generation. Loosely defined as success, no measurable yardsticks were in place to provide a precise definition.

Carving out a distinct individuality is characteristic of success. In Shazia's case, her unabashed public smoking lent her that ability. It was uncommon for girls to smoke in public; the common perception linked the habit to absence of morality. However, for men, smoking was considered just a bad habit. Shazia's male colleagues found it intriguing, therefore, when she held a cigarette defiantly between her fingers, puffing away. They waited for the moment when she pouted her lips to blow away the smoke up towards the ceiling. These frustrated souls felt blessed to inhale her smoke; each puff offering a climax of its own. But what exasperated them was the ease with which she conversed with everyone without any hint of intimacy. Their advances would be met by a cold stare. And for the more intrusive, her scowl would be enough.

Farid Khan was infatuated. Ever since he had joined the new bank, he just couldn't take his eyes off Shazia, glancing at her whenever he could from the safety of his cubicle. He had noticed her for the first time at a corporate dinner. The image stuck in his mind was of her sitting around a bonfire, holding the neckband of her white jumper, engaged in discussion.

In a few weeks, the weather changed, and Lahore started getting warm. Shazia started wearing slim-fitted half-sleeved shirts and formal trousers. Although summers offered a better view of her well-toned physique, the image of the jumper was etched in Farid's mind. Although they had been formally introduced to each other in the office, being part of separate teams, their contact remained minimal. It was only when a mutual friend and colleague, Hassan, invited them to a weekend party, masquerading as dinner, that they got introduced to each other more intimately.

* * *

Hassan's borrowed motto of work hard and party hard had now become the local mantra, and the basement of his house was ideally laid out for revellers. The crowd was largely made up of young professionals—bankers, and marketing and finance executives. With a separate entrance leading to the basement, Hassan's guests enjoyed the loudest of parties without interfering with the sensibilities of the neighbours. The basement opened out into an open area separated by a sliding double-glazed glass door. A staircase from the basement led up towards the back lawn on the ground floor.

Hassan, as always, had carefully planned the event, ensuring a balanced gender ratio. His parties were the talk of the town, prompting the omnipresent gatecrashers to try and get past the heavy security at the entrance. Even television celebrities and cricket players were known to attend. But this time it was only friends and close acquaintances. It was a Saturday evening, and by 10 p.m., the basement was teeming with young people. They were all dressed in the trendiest clothes. Amid the din, one could overhear stray pieces of conversation—all in English. The objective of having conversation at such parties was not to communicate, but to impress the other with the fluency of a borrowed language. At these places, the pronunciation indicated the upbringing of a person. While mispronunciation of the local language was tossed aside as unimportant, eyebrows were raised where English was concerned.

The experienced DJ, who had been especially flown in from Karachi, interacted with the audience by speaking in phrases aimed at bringing out the Dionysian spirit to its fullest. The crowd reciprocated by flailing its arms amid loud cheers. The well-stocked bar was mobbed by the guests yearning to get into the mood. The strobe light kept flashing up the dance floor, appearing to freeze the movements of the enthusiastic dancers. It was an ingenious way of hiding the participants' limited dancing talent without dampening their fervour. An effusive blue light highlighted the colour white, making it glow. It was here that Farid saw Shazia, resplendent in a white top, walk out of the glass door.

'You don't dance?' Shazia asked Farid as he came and sat beside her on the lawn.

'No, I don't, but I like the frenzy.'

'So, is this your cigarette break?'

'Yes, kind of. It was getting warm in there. Did you have something to drink?' she asked.

'Yes, I am having one.' Farid showed her the bottle he was holding. 'Murree beer is the best. I prefer it to all the European beers. Do you want to have one?'

'Yes, if you could get me one, please.'

Though Farid had asked hesitatingly, Shazia's prompt acceptance came as a surprise.

Farid brought her a chilled bottle and, they toasted before Shazia took a sip.

'Hassan has planted some fruit trees here,' Shazia remarked, looking around.

'Yes, that one is grapefruit; makes good juice in summers. We have grown a number of these trees at our village,' Farid pointed at one of the many trees planted in a line near the boundary wall.

'And what is the name of your village?'

'Charbagh.'

'Charbagh,' Shazia repeated and glanced at Farid.

'Where is Charbagh?'

'District Mardan.'

'You mean next to Tarbela Dam,' Shazia seemed to know the place.

'Yes. Why, have you been there?'
'Not really. I heard the name from someone.'

* * *

The coming week saw some changes at the bank;
Farid and Shazia ended up in the same team. Their
first assignment was to attend a lenders' meeting at a
cement factory in Chakwal. Instead of opting for the
office car, Farid took his personal vehicle and Shazia
accompanied him. On their way back, while still
far from the motorway, he asked Shazia if she was
interested in shooting.
'Where?'
'Well, right here. We can stop here and shoot at a
target in a field.'
Shazia wasn't sure but Farid did not give her a lot
of time to contemplate the offer. He took out the black
box from under his seat and proudly showed off his
handgun—it was the same model he had bought for
Imran. After giving her some basic instructions on its
mechanism, he loaded it and pointed at a stone at the
edge of a wheat field for her to shoot. Though she was
not able to hit the target, Shazia seemed to control the
recoil better than expected. The fact that she emptied
the fourteen-bullet charger without exaggerated
flinching was pleasantly surprising for Farid. While
she was aiming at the stone, Farid kept caressing his
moustache, appreciating her sinewy arms. Her poise,

with her feet firmly perched on the ground and her arms extended forward, made him fantasize about those muscular legs caressing her trousers, making him terribly excited.

On their way back, Shazia asked him the reason for carrying a gun. Farid was cautious, saying it was part of a long tradition.

'We feel incomplete without one,' Farid boasted.

'Why should one need a gun to feel complete? Don't you trust yourself?'

'But I cannot trust this distorted society. One never knows what goes on in the minds of the people here. One has to be careful.'

And then Farid enumerated various incidents— some overheard, others exaggerated—faced by his family and friends over several years where a gun had come in handy. His justification didn't seem to impress Shazia.

* * *

Naveed and Farid were bosom buddies. Friends since preparatory school, their relationship had survived the tumult of time, maturing from milk to beer. Their rendezvous was usually at Naveed's place, who had bought a house tucked away in a corner of Defence Housing Authority, specifically for their weekend escapades. While Naveed had got married at a young age, Farid strongly believed he was not meant for a permanent relationship. It was a weekend, and Farid, in his laconic manner, had let Naveed know about Shazia.

'Farid Khan, why bother about her? Everything is available in this city. Enjoy your life without getting involved.' Farid was in deep contemplation, staring at the front wall, as Naveed handed him a bottle of beer.

'I know, but this is different,' Farid's voice seemed to echo from somewhere deep within.

During the past few years, Farid had come across a couple of girls, but the relationships could not survive the test of his ego. At one time, he had been put off by a girl who had refused to let him photograph her. Farid was offended and never spoke to her again. At another instance, the fact that the girl he was dating had danced with someone he despised had enraged him. Without listening to any explanations, he had dumped her unceremoniously from his car at the parking lot in Gymkhana. She kept telling him, 'But you don't dance, and we were in a group.' But he had paid no heed and screeched out of the club.

And then there was a darker side to his egotistical self. Only last year, on his way to Charbagh from Lahore, a BMW on the motorway wasn't letting him overtake. Farid tried to overtake from the right, displaying his indicator, but it didn't budge. He then tried to overtake from the left, only to find the BMW increase its speed to frustrate him. Farid was furious. He saw the driver mock him by slapping the hand of another occupant in the front seat. The black box carrying his gun was beside him on the front seat. Holding the car handle with one hand, he pulled out the gun. He rolled down the window on the right and looked into the rear-view mirror first. The car behind him was too far to notice anything. With no other traffic in view except the BMW speeding in the right lane, he loaded his gun. Without an overt display of bravado, he protruded his hand just a little and fired. As the bullet shattered the back screen, the BMW careened sharply towards the left, cutting across the breadth of the motorway, and tumbled several times towards the green area. Without stopping, Farid looked back and saw it come to a halt against one of the eucalyptus trees. There was a triumphant smile on his face as he put away the gun.

Farid's attitude made it difficult to forge a lasting relationship with any girl. From time to time, Naveed would introduce him to women for temporary liaisons. Naveed had convinced him that the myth that all women were alike was contrived by the impotent. Every woman was different in her own right; she just needed to be explored appropriately to bring out the passion in her. With all kinds available at a price, Naveed didn't see the need to get into trouble with girls from secure backgrounds. He would often advise Farid, 'The odds of a chase ending up in disappointment are greater as compared to the anticipated pleasure.' Naveed spoke on these issues with authority and from experience. For Farid, the positive side of these temporary liaisons was the honesty with which each transaction was carried out. But there was always something lacking, something he couldn't express with words. He looked forward to every liaison with excitement, but it always ended up making him even more frustrated. Every tryst, instead of fulfilling his desire, increased his dissatisfaction. He had expressed this emptiness to Naveed, especially the post-tryst depression, who instead asked him to enjoy life and count its blessings. Unable to understand Farid's urge for ultimate satisfaction, Naveed would tell him in his characteristically persuasive manner, 'A woman is the highest pleasure known to man. For ultimate satisfaction, wait till we go to heaven.'

After meeting Shazia, for the first time, Farid believed he had found someone he could forge a longer relationship with. He appreciated her nonchalant manner. Nothing seemed to perturb her, not even shortage of stock at a customer's godown. She could deal with any situation and handle any boss. And he loved the way Shazia stretched her mouth to emphasize a specific word. This habit, picked up from American movies, kicked up his physical longing for her.

Naveed tried talking Farid out of his obsession with Shazia but failed. Every time they talked about Shazia, to Naveed's frustration, Farid would start stroking his moustache, conveying his resolve. A man of few words, he did not like getting into discussions.

Meanwhile, corporate life offered little time for leisure. Even weekends were sometimes spent in sorting out client issues. Given the nature of their work, Farid and Shazia spent a lot of time together, including travelling to other cities. On their return, they would come back to the office where Shazia would pick up her car and go home. But on that particular day, she hadn't brought her car, and on returning from a day trip, asked Farid to drop her off at her residence. They had been in the same team for almost six months now, a long enough time to develop a level of comfort with each other. Shazia kept giving him directions till they reached an enormous wall, outlining a large residential area. Shazia asked him to approach the gate and put off the headlights. Although a large number of gated communities had sprung up in the city, the size of the wall and the gate was awe-inspiring. A heavily armed guard stepped outside. By that time Shazia had put the cabin light on, making it easier for him to identify the occupants. He smiled at her and gestured to someone inside to open the gate. As he drove in, Farid found himself in a lush green, artfully decorated garden surrounded by residences. Shazia asked Farid to take a right and stop in front of a house. Shazia took out a scarf from her handbag and covered her head with it as she prepared to get down. But what really surprised Farid was *Charbagh House* written in large fonts on a board at her entrance. As he turned towards her in astonishment, she had already guessed his question.

'Yes, I know. Charbagh House. Now I am tired, will tell you tomorrow.' She smiled and before Farid could ask her anything, she nimbly jumped out of the car.

The next day, Farid eagerly waited to meet Shazia after office hours. He was deeply intrigued to understand her Charbagh connection. After a never-ending day, finally they were able to meet at a coffee shop. Seeing Farid's expectant look, Shazia immediately came to the point.

'We belong to Charbagh. Yes, your Charbagh. Our family lived there for several generations. My grandfather converted and became an Ahmadi or Qadiani, whatever you want to call them. And I leave it to your judgement if you consider us Muslims or not. Anyway, from that time onwards, there was animosity in the village against our family. But it simmered somewhere beneath the surface. We never came to know about it. Yes, there were some families who did not want to socialize with us, but that was their choice and we respected it. There was no major upheaval in our lives till such time that a bill was passed in the National Assembly, identifying us as non-Muslims. Soon after the passage of that bill we realized the changing attitudes of Charbagh's residents. Most of the families started boycotting us. My father tells me that only a few families in the entire village were left who socialized with us—all Ahmadis. So, we sought comfort with each other, believing things would calm down over a period of time. We had land and we just couldn't leave it. There was a maulana there, who added fuel to the fire. I don't remember his name, but he was the one who instigated people against us. The denunciation of our community became a regular feature of his sermons until it reached a boiling point. A charged mob attacked and burnt our homes, and killed some of our community members. Luckily, my parents and I were not in the village on that day. In a single night we became refugees. But my father could not forget his roots and despite the horrid experience, named our house Charbagh. That is the only connection left with our ancestral village now.'

Farid was dumbfounded. Both were quiet for a long time. Not knowing what to say, he suddenly asked her, 'Do you speak Pushto?'

'Not really. After we left the village, my parents stopped speaking the language. We made a fresh start in Lahore.'

'And the place where you live?'

'Yes, the compound where you dropped me off is the last place in Lahore where so many people from our community live together.'

After this candid disclosure, Farid squirmed with desire for Shazia. He felt a stronger urge to get close to her physically. The shared background worked as a catalyst for his fantasies, where they roamed the streets of Charbagh holding hands, sat under the trees eating mangoes, went out for partridge hunts together, and finally after a long day, made uninhibited love in his room at the mansion. He imagined her toned body pressed against his in passionate love and strongly believed only Shazia could provide that wholesome experience he was lacking. The girls he had been with until then were like partridges: he could shoot them at will. But with her, he was physically and mentally inspired. She brought out a kind of excitement he had never felt for anyone before. And now, having found out that she was a non-Muslim, the anticipation of pleasure knew no bounds.

Through his village connections, Farid tried to find out more about her. He was told that they had a small landholding in the village. Her father was an air cargo pilot with the air force and had died recently. The family formed an insignificant part of the village. Given that Shazia was a non-Muslim, there couldn't be a formal arrangement unless she agreed to convert. But asking someone to change their belief was not a simple proposition. What if she asked him to do the same? But Farid wasn't prepared to commit to a lifetime of misery anyway. He kept thinking about the relationship. They could live together, he thought. Such arrangements were being worked out by bold couples in Karachi, but Lahore was still rural and thereby more conservative. People loved to snoop around for affairs. Even if they couldn't find any, they concocted one. It made for good gossip. For all practical purposes, it was a tough proposition to live with an Ahmadi girl in Lahore, without invoking religious backlash.

* * *

A year passed but Farid, besides giving some occasional hints through his body language, couldn't find the right opportunity to tell Shazia how much he wanted her. He was mesmerized by her. On one occasion, as he dropped her off at her residence, she mentioned, 'Thanks, Farid. We have become good friends now. By the way, my mother wanted me to give you something. Come on in for a while.'

It was the first time she had invited him to her house. The drawing room represented an average Pakistani household but was remarkably clean. As Farid looked around, there were no objects to indicate the religious background of its inhabitants. The only object of interest was a large black-and-white family photograph, in which Shazia's father sat confidently in his air force uniform at one end of the sofa. Her mother, a plain-looking woman with large glasses, sat beside him with her hands in her lap. Her two brothers sat beside their mother, while a pre-teen Shazia stood with a cheeky smile on her face, as if mocking the photographer. Farid realized that Shazia's long upper lip and sharp jawline was a replica of her father's; and for her height she needed to thank both her parents. As he sat interpreting the rest of her features, Shazia entered with a booklet in her hands.

'My mother wanted me to give you this booklet of daily prayers. It carries prayers for all occasions. My mother likes praying for my friends. Ever since I told her about you, she prays for you and wants you to pray for her as well.'

Farid thanked her and left. He wasn't too keen on reading the prayer book and left it in the dashboard of his car. His mind was occupied with deciphering the meaning of 'good friends', as she had called him. He was sure about one thing: he didn't want to belong to the reductive category of a friend. He wanted a tangible relationship, albeit a physical one.

Over the months, as they got even closer, Shazia never stopped mentioning how comfortable she felt in his company. On various occasions, she would hug him and tell him how important friends were in life. He looked forward to those moments, considering them to be steps leading towards the final episode of a serious relationship. But these moments seemed to drag on, without leading anywhere; they were losing their excitement.

Farid wanted her physically, and a time came when he reached the end of his patience. While he never practised abstinence, as required by his faith, he believed other religions didn't lay out any stringent moral codes. For him, morality was strictly confined to the followers of his faith only. So, on Naveed's persuasion, Farid took Shazia to their hideout. He had waited too long and now wanted to make things clear. As they sat on the sofa, Farid took her hand and expressed in his own terse manner how much he looked forward to being intimate with her.

'Look, Farid, I have always considered you a good friend. Anything beyond that will destroy our friendship.'

'Have I acted in any way to lose your trust?' Farid murmured.

'No, you haven't until now. But the fact that you brought me here, to this unknown place, makes me very uncomfortable.'

'Can't friends have feelings for each other? Why do men and women get married in the first place?' Farid's logic was simple.

'Farid, I have always considered you a friend. In fact, you are the best friend I have.'

Farid ignored her remark and continued, 'Let me make it simple for you. You want to guard your freedom and I appreciate that. We will not get married. But let us live together as a couple.' Farid finally conveyed his physical desire for Shazia in so many words.

'Farid, what makes you think we can live together without getting married? It is so wayward. And you know we cannot get married in the first place. I have never even thought about it.'

'Why, you don't like me?'

'Yes, I do.'

'Then, what is the issue?'

'Look Farid,' she clasped his hand. 'Why do you want to destroy this lovely relationship? I feel so safe and secure in your presence. Our circumstances are different. I live alone with my mother. Both my brothers are abroad. She needs me. I do not want to commit myself physically and emotionally at this stage.

Please try to understand. I have never even considered you from that angle. Let us be friends, best friends. Now, please let us go.'

Left high and dry, Farid's face was flushed with anger and humiliation. His carefully nurtured fantasy had collapsed in a single conversation, and he sat staring at the floor. Shazia was also in a very difficult situation. Here she was with her supposedly best friend, desperately trying to make him understand the existence and importance of platonic relationships.

Farid drove rashly on the way back, and she did not stop him. Shazia knew he was offended and kept quiet. She had always admired Farid for his quiet charisma and strong personality. She always believed he was someone who would be there in her time of need. But she could not imagine having a physical relationship with him, not even as a husband. What else could she call him but a friend?

Farid wasn't sure how to respond as the blood of Charbagh within him boiled with anger. He had all sorts of images floating in his head. When he started sifting through them to find options, there were none. Perhaps Naveed would have an answer.

* * *

'Have you ever exchanged anything?' Naveed asked him. Farid had asked Naveed to meet in the evening the next day. Naveed was surprised since it was not a weekend.

Farid thought for a while. 'I bought her a perfume once and got her some sweets from the village. That's about it.'

'Did she ever give you anything?'

'A pen once.'

'Not good enough. Anything else?'

'A book of daily prayers, but that is not important.'

'A book of prayers,' Naveed repeated. 'Where is it? I want to see it.'

The book was still lying untouched in the dashboard. Farid went to the car and handed it over to Naveed. As he opened the first page, he looked at it for a while and then smiled.

'Farid Khan, we got what we wanted. Printed in Rabwah, do you see that? And it has her address as well.'

'Yes, so what?' Farid replied, unimpressed with Naveed's discovery.

'Will let you know tomorrow. You are on leave for a couple of days, right? So be ready at 11 a.m.'

* * *

It was Friday, and Shazia was looking forward to a relaxed weekend. After work, she had gone straight to the market to buy her mother some toiletries, which somehow couldn't wait for Saturday. As she came out, there were four police officers along with a lady officer waiting for her.

'Madam, are you Ms Shazia?'

'Yes, I am.'

'You have to come with us. There is an arrest warrant against you.'

The introverted Farid Khan had shown his spots and in doing so, had exposed the insidiousness of the feudal mindset. Naveed's devious plan had worked. His contacts had helped him in laying one of the most savage traps one could imagine. A trap no one could ever imagine getting out of in this country. The booklet of prayers Shazia had presented to Farid was utilized in implicating her. The charge against her read, 'For spreading the banned Qadiani faith and undermining the established religion.' The first information report filed with the police implicated the entire locality where Shazia lived with spreading their banned faith by enticing innocent men like Farid Khan. The report mentioned her action as a crime against the state and prayed for strict punishment against her. She was held firmly by her arm as she was led towards the police car; the charges brought up were enough to result in a death sentence.

10

Mahbanu

Fort Munro was a huge disappointment in every sense of the word. There was no fort; the only structure present was a brick-and-mortar sarcophagus, called Deputy Commissioner's Residence. Located in the Solomon Mountain range, Fort Munro, until christened, was just a peak among many, albeit the highest in South Punjab. Even if it were the lowest, the British would have concocted some way of heaping glory upon themselves. What did one expect the peak of an arid mountain range to contain? Absolutely nothing, right? And there was, in fact, nothing at the top. So, the entire blame once again rested with the British, especially the Anglo-Saxons among them, who in their lust for conquest had sought to build a kingdom as extensive as that of King Solomon. The vantage point at Fort Munro was duly baptized by the colonists, leaving behind four graves of some adventurous family; one of them was of a child who must have passed away due to the acute disappointment at the horrible realization. The best part about the British was their penchant for documentation: the epitaphs provided the details of the buried. Encased in iron grills, the graves were firmly protected from indigenous curiosity.

Mahbanu was furious. On the way down to the plains, she kept arguing with her husband, Amir, for wasting a beautiful winter's day. The poor army major, who had borrowed a diesel Toyota Corolla from his friend for the trip, tried to calm her by pointing out the positives, but Mahbanu's mood could not be elevated. Amir and Mahbanu were one of those rare couples who had fallen in love after marriage. Now together for almost six months, he couldn't thank his mother more for having discovered this gem of a Baloch girl. The symmetry of Mahbanu's oval face and the delicacy of those calm features made her beautiful. It was the first time Amir had seen her frown, and he couldn't take his eyes off her.

'Don't look at me, please keep your eyes on the road.' Mahbanu couldn't seem to get over her disappointment.

'I will never go with the judgement of an army man! And what did your friend tell you exactly?'

'That Fort Munro is six and a half thousand feet above sea level and that it is the summer capital of South Punjab.' Amir parroted the fact as a child would in front of his teacher in a classroom.

'And that one could get a chance to meet the Chief Djinn of King Solomon's personal security as well,' Amir quipped.

'Oh, for God's sake! Why are you army men so obsessed with measurements? If I had the authority, I would have thrown this friend of yours out of the army and enclosed him in one of those graves up there.'

'How could you be so cruel? A graduate of liberal arts, a connoisseur of art, a painter! Even your cruelty is creative!' Amir smiled and glanced at her.

'At least wear a seat belt. It might contain your disappointment.' Amir couldn't help glancing sideways, suppressing his smile. Mahbanu's skin gleamed in the golden rays of the setting sun, and the prominent dimple on her sharp chin further enhanced her appeal.

* * *

The images were all mixed up. She saw some rough-looking people bending over her. Suddenly they disappeared and she saw another bunch of men and women draped in white, wearing masks. The sounds were all so confusing as well; Balochi suddenly replaced by a mixture of refined English and Urdu. There was a lot of movement around her. Unusual sounds like some machines being put to work unwillingly. And then it was all quiet as all the images slowly faded away.

She was awakened by someone pressing her hand. It was her mother. Her eyes were red and swollen, and she smiled and thanked Allah when Mahbanu looked at her. She couldn't fully understand what her mother meant when she asked, 'How are you feeling, my child?' Why was this question being put to her? Slowly regaining consciousness, she recalled the last moments before the blackout. It was a steep descent on a winding road, and there were no safety barriers at any turn. She could remember constantly telling Amir not to glance at her and keep his eyes on the road. That was the last she remembered. She couldn't comprehend her current situation. Instead of Amir, she was with her mother, and the car had transformed into a room. As she tried to move, she realized there was no sensation in her legs. But before she could say anything, she slipped back into induced sleep.

* * *

It had been one week since her accident. The prognosis was bleak. Apart from a broken shoulder blade and collarbone, she had been left paralysed below the waist. But there was hope. She was moved to the Orthopaedic Excellence Centre at the Combined Military Hospital in Rawalpindi to give her a second chance at life.

At Rawalpindi, in a matter of six months, Mahbanu went through two operations on her spine. Then, she had to undergo four months of physiotherapy. Even after these stages of re-embodiment, she couldn't stand on her feet. The doctors and nurses had given her their best. She realized that despite all its claims, scientific development had its limits. She might be limited to spending her whole life in bed.

Surprisingly, Amir had only suffered minor injuries and was on duty after a week. While Mahbanu was at the hospital in Multan, Amir made sure he spent all his time with her after office hours. But once Mahbanu was transferred to Rawalpindi, it became difficult for him to fly in every weekend. A major in the army didn't have the financial resources to travel by commercial airline on a weekly basis, and military planes were not available very frequently. Luckily, Mahbanu's parents and her only sibling, Asim, were stationed in Rawalpindi. Her father, a retired army officer, and her mother, a supportive housewife, were too advanced in years to take care of her; so, the responsibility fell on Asim's shoulders. The dutiful young man practically gave up his studies to look after Mahbanu.

'I have asked for a sympathetic transfer to Rawalpindi, but it will take time. Army has its own procedures.' Amir told Mahbanu that his commanding officer knew about the incident and would help him get the transfer at the earliest. The summary for his transfer would soon be signed. As a sizeable military force, they just couldn't send personnel around at the snap of a finger. She didn't have a reason not to believe Amir.

The hospital stay was relatively easy, and she had doctors and nurses to take care of her every minute. The objective at the time was to make her sit up in a wheelchair. Mahbanu dreaded the day she would be discharged and made to face a life she had never dreamt of even in her wildest imagination. Going forward, she rightly believed it to be a life of drudgery. The thought kept her awake most of the nights.

After a year of physical therapy, Mahbanu finally managed to sit upright in bed. It was such a joyous occasion when she had her first meal by herself sitting upright. Her parents and brother just couldn't stop laughing and chatting as they sat around her in the room. Her father kept reminding her of Allah's love and her Baloch resolve.

Mahbanu had rightly anticipated life to be a struggle. The normal actions of rising from bed and getting ready for the day were nothing less than a project. She felt so helpless and unfortunate while carrying out these daily rituals. The muscles in her shoulders hurt so much that it was impossible for her to even brush her hair without help. A full-time nurse had to be employed to take care of her.

Meanwhile, Asim had rejoined his university after having taken a gap year for the sake of his sister. Now it was her parents who had to manage the needs of their frail daughter. But this time it was different from when she was a child. With their own health on the wane, Mahbanu's needs—physical and emotional—were entirely different, and the grief in their eyes was visible. Her father refused to believe that she was paraplegic, constantly insisting that she needed to mentally believe in her ability to walk. She could see his frustration when despite her best efforts she couldn't. He would put his hands on her shoulders and say, 'Yes, we will make it happen. Where is your Baloch stubbornness?' She could only simper at his naivete, appreciating an ex-soldier's resolve.

Meanwhile, another year passed by. Amir's visits became less frequent. Sympathy has a short life and gets fatigued easily. His weekly visits became monthly, and then a time came when he would speak to Mahbanu over the phone once a month. His assurances of a transfer to Rawalpindi never materialized. With each passing day, his tone started getting more detached. And then, she started hearing rumours of his second marriage. She pointedly asked him over the phone call, but he denied them, assuring her of his unending love. But the rumours didn't end, making her nervous and depressed. When pushed to visit her, he would come up with the most convincing excuse to wriggle out of it. He portrayed himself as though he were the only bulwark against terrorists in the province of Punjab. With a gloomy tone he would say, 'It is a miracle that I am still alive.' He constantly asked her to pray for his safety. Mahbanu sincerely believed Amir still loved her. In the brief six months of their marriage before the accident, he had always reminded her how lucky he was to have her as a wife. And then one day, she received a registered mail from Amir. Duly addressed to her, it contained her divorce papers. There was a poignant letter as well, asking for forgiveness. Amir seemed to have won the war against terrorists.

* * *

Maulana Ishaq was a government-paid imam in a small mosque in Lahore. His entire life circled around going to the mosque, leading prayers and facing his nagging wife in a small two-bedroom flat. With five mouths to feed, he always felt that the compensation for taking care of God's house was not equivalent to the effort. In the fifteen years of this assignment, he had consistently tried to get a transfer to one of the larger mosques but could not find an opportunity. Government-controlled mosques offered lifelong careers, albeit in the same position and without any prospects of better facilities. However, a large mosque had the potential to provide higher personal donations from a larger pool of worshippers. With the construction of new mosques limited due to constrained budgets, the only prospect for fresh vacancies rose when an incumbent either retired at sixty or was recalled by the Divine. And so, with no promotion, increase in salary or substantive donations to look forward to, Maulana Ishaq's religious enthusiasm was always at its lowest ebb. He demonstrated this by keeping the prayers as short as possible, getting them over with in a hurried manner and dismissing any questions from the followers. It was only when invited to speak in larger mosques or gatherings that he felt energized. As his eyes swept across these crowds, he felt a surge of passion overtake his sacred sensibilities. With absolute disregard towards any entity, spiritual or physical, he tended to direct his disillusionment at the government, with the sole objective of building up his own brand. He attempted to drive a wedge between the public and the government, pointing out the waywardness of the rulers. His sharp tongue and incisive wit resonated with the crowds in the way that he wanted. He successfully projected his will at these crowds by constantly asking them to either raise their hands in favour of his argument or chant slogans supporting his stance. While his peers were mindful of their language, Ishaq felt no qualms. People thoroughly enjoyed the street expletives intertwined with religious texts that he employed. His black turban, swollen lips and constant frown gave him a distinctive look, further enhancing his brand value. He understood the fickleness of the general public, who in the time of social media required a constant dose of dopamine. In time, he came to be known as the saviour of the Ummah, the nation of Islam.

Maulana Ishaq carefully chose subjects that would create a commotion. Unlike his peers who stuck to religious topics, he took up issues that were political in nature, requiring minimal religious knowledge, thereby cleverly hiding his ignorance. With his viewership on YouTube constantly on the rise, Ishaq had now become a celebrity in his own right. People from various cities invited him for sermons, knowing his star power. Such gatherings attracted large donations as well, of which the maulana received a large proportion from the organizers, further swelling his lips and accentuating his frown. A time came when he viewed his salary as pocket money for his children and he secretly confided to his closest friends that his wife's nagging had surprisingly converted into confessions of love for him. His large mouth would split into a wide grin unveiling the meat stuck between his crooked teeth.

To maintain his new-found source of income and star status, the maulana neglected the small mosque allotted to him. He asked his son to lead the prayers during his perpetual absence. His non-attendance and antics were noted by the government department officials. A show-cause notice was issued, to which he never bothered to respond. Various reminders were sent, which remained unanswered as well. Instead, in his sermons, he severely criticized the secular governmental set-ups and even denounced the Constitution of the country as un-Islamic. Faced with no other option, the government dismissed him from service.

Maulana Ishaq was on the Grand Trunk Road, travelling from Gujranwala to Lahore, when he received a call informing him of his dismissal. Furious, in his characteristic manner, he heaped the choicest of expletives upon the government, startling his driver.

The moral digression was too much for the poor driver to ingest.

* * *

Meanwhile, Mahbanu didn't see a good reason for her to live any more. She couldn't recall any delinquency meriting this response from fate. What had the universe gained by putting her in a wheelchair? What she was supposed to do now was murky as well. With nowhere to escape, she kept wondering why the soul just didn't slip out of the body and set her free. Why did it require a grievous injury to the body for the soul to be separated from the body? Alternately, why couldn't an injury to the soul result in amicable separation between the two entities? The way Amir had treated her hurt deep inside. But despite the physical advancement of humans, there were no parameters defined for measuring the condition of a soul. Even her psychiatrist never referred to this living entity. To Mahbanu, the basic problem originated from putting together the physical with the metaphysical: two eternally different entities forcefully put together. This was the thought process she was going through when her father came up with a proposition.

'Mahbanu, my friend has a school for the under-privileged in Chak Shahzad, Islamabad.'

Short on choices, Mahbanu started teaching English grammar and reading to the girls and boys of classes

six and seven. Her father had arranged for a driver
as well. Despite her painful daily struggle, Mahbanu
found something in her life to look forward to. She
started wearing shirts and trousers as she had done
prior to the accident. With her straight hair neatly
hanging over her shoulders, Mahbanu didn't have the
persona of a teacher; she looked more like a model.
Her propensity to wear colourful clothes, accessorized
with a scarf, added to her glamour quotient.

Initially her fellow teachers pitied her and asked
her lots of personal questions, which made her
uncomfortable. But her propensity to smile and ability
to politely evade personal intrusion made her popular.
Given her depth of knowledge and clarity of thought,
they were charmed by her and started calling her madam.

It so happened that a United Nations delegation
visited the school since it was being promoted as a
model school. The principal felt that Mahbanu was the
obvious choice to coordinate with the delegation. They
were so impressed by her presentation that they asked
her to become their Goodwill Ambassador for Women
in the country. Having received this recognition, doors
to stardom opened for her. She started being invited
by various non-government organizations and private
institutions as a motivational speaker.

In her first motivational speech, Mahbanu was
dumbfounded. She didn't know what to say. An
accident had taken place, resulting in a broken body.
She struggled to spend a single painless day. Just

when she needed her loved ones, the most important person in her life had left her unceremoniously. But then there were millions like her in the country who had suffered more than her, but none could become a motivational speaker.

Her merit was the fluency of the language in which she spoke: English. What other credentials did she have? Yes, she also had the finesse and compassion to go with the language, which made a difference. Those attendees of her sessions, who moments ago had despised her for moving around in a wheelchair, portraying herself to be a victim of fate, were moved by her straight and honest talk. She never claimed anything, didn't blame anything, didn't hate anyone, but had a message of hope for everyone.

Mahbanu made it a point to visit patients in hospitals, especially the ones involved in serious accidents, and talked to them about their future plans. Her soft and dulcet tone had such a therapeutic impact on the patients that the city hospitals started contacting her to pep up their patients whenever required.

* * *

Maulana Ishaq was badly injured in the accident. While the driver was quickly disposed of into the ground in a short religious ceremony, the followers of the maulana ensured that he received the best medical care available in Lahore. Unfortunately, his well-wishers couldn't support his spine and the maulana was finally declared a paraplegic.

Confined to his wheelchair, the maulana took a turn for the worst. Having survived death, he became even more abusive. The story circulated by his supporters was of a conspiracy theory: the state wanted him killed but by Allah's mercy he had survived. They believed his survival in a physically diminished form was evidence of the Divine affirmation of his brand. With limited mobility, the maulana now had to find something quickly that could help him remain relevant in the temporal. And then there was a God-sent opportunity. Days after the maulana was discharged from the hospital in a wheelchair, Junaid's blasphemy case—splashed all across the county on various news channels and social media for the past many years—reached its conclusion when the Supreme Court found Junaid mentally unfit to face trial, meaning that he could be set free. The opportune time to take action had arrived. The maulana jumped to grab the opportunity before some other religious party could snatch it away from him. He hurriedly called his confidantes for a meeting, and after brief deliberations, announced a grand sit-in at Faizabad, at the junction of Rawalpindi and Islamabad.

* * *

It was chaos as traffic between the twin cities of Rawalpindi and Islamabad came to a stop. The junction at Faizabad overflowed with people supporting the cause of Maulana Ishaq. They came from all over the country. Many locals were willing to cater to their brothers in arms by providing them warm clothing and food. The law enforcement agencies let the maulana carry out his will by keeping a safe distance from him and his supporters. Only the traffic police were called out in large numbers to manage the mile-long traffic jams at diversions. People were greatly inconvenienced as they tried to work around this religious extravaganza.

The sit-in had one purpose: to force the judiciary to hang Junaid to death. Maulana Ishaq and his followers firmly believed Junaid to be a culprit who must be hanged for blasphemy, even though mentally disabled. According to their argument, the blasphemy was committed when he was mentally sound. They also believed him to be feigning mental incapacity to escape punishment. Any thought of releasing him was, therefore, considered sacrilegious. Releasing Junaid meant a win for the secular and liberal forces, while death meant a win for the cause of religion. The maulana was blunt in his tirade against the government. He threatened to storm the jail in which Junaid was incarcerated, if the culprit was not hanged.

Coverage across the media was extensive. Day in and day out they showed a defiant maulana surrounded by his henchmen, ready to kill or be killed for the just cause that he represented. Several television anchors interviewed him over the course of the week of the sit-in.

Some pleaded with him to clear up the area so that people could continue with their lives, but he remained defiant. When they pointed out the suffering caused to patients who could not reach the hospitals or the children who missed their schools, the maulana saw this as a minor sacrifice for the cause of religion. He would bark at the anchors, 'You want me to abandon a greater cause for the sake of minor inconvenience to the public? You should be ashamed of yourselves. In fact, your place is here. You should become part of this sit-in.' So, they stopped interviewing him, showing visuals only while covering the news.

* * *

For the past week, Mahbanu had desperately tried to attend her school. On two separate days she had got stuck for almost seven hours in the traffic. Her body couldn't bear such exertion. She could barely get up for the next three days. On Monday, the situation remained the same, bringing misery upon misery to the locals. She left her house again but not to go to school; she was determined to do something more worthwhile.

As Mahbanu's car reached close to the venue of the sit-in, she asked to be taken to Maulana Ishaq. Though her driver and nurse advised her against it, she remained adamant. Reluctantly, both helped her to the wheelchair, and the nurse reluctantly pushed her towards the sit-in. Mahbanu brusquely brushed aside the flimsy police cordon, asking her nurse not to stop. The crowds of ever-present onlookers readily let her wheelchair pass. The hordes comprised a large number of women and children as well, who stood there anticipating some breakthrough in the daily negotiations between the government and the maulana. A large television screen was already set up near the sit-in, which prior to this drama was showing advertisements. It took Mahbanu almost twenty minutes to reach the maulana. As Mahbanu's wheelchair moved forward, the appearance of the sit-in participants grew increasingly ferocious. While the outer parameter was occupied by repulsive characters, the core around the maulana comprised thugs. The expression on those coarse-looking faces was anything but pious. This was a bunch of hardened criminals claiming to be the defenders of a peaceful religion.

Abdul Aziz was standing right behind Maulana Ishaq when he saw the two women move towards them. He left his place and stood in front of him, stopping the two some ten steps away. Mahbanu insisted on seeing the maulana, which he declined. By this time, the various television cameras had spotted something of interest. For the past one week, all television stations had been relaying a direct telecast of the sit-in across the country. So, the viewers were curious when they saw a young, modern-looking girl in a wheelchair arguing with a bearded man. All the onlookers were glued to their screens, trying to find out what exactly this girl was up to. While Mahbanu was arguing with Abdul Aziz, another of the maulana's bodyguards came up from behind. Having understood the situation, he quickly moved back to the maulana, also seated in his wheelchair, and conveyed the intention of the lady. The eyes of the maulana lit up for a split second. He shouted to Abdul Aziz to let her come near.

Maulana Ishaq saw a presentable young lady, modern in appearance but confined to a wheelchair, move closer. In a red jacket and a colourful scarf, Mahbanu seemed to be dressed for the occasion. His first reaction was to ask his people to get her something so she could cover her hair. Abdul Aziz took the chador from his shoulder and tried to throw it over her head, which she forcefully pushed away.

'Maulana sahib,' Mahbanu's voice shook with emotion, 'I want to talk to you as an equal. I don't ask you to remove your turban, so you shouldn't insist that I cover my hair.'

Reluctantly, the maulana beckoned Abdul Aziz to step aside. She moved even closer to the maulana. Meanwhile, live television kept streaming from the venue of the sit-in. Mahbanu's driver joined the people in watching the large screen as he saw his madam approach the maulana. The crowd seemed to go quiet. All television anchors had their own take on the identity of this lady and her intention. Maulana Ishaq was visibly uneasy; his swollen lips had protruded more and his frown had deepened. As he studied her face, his eyes rested on the dimple on her chin, the definitive mark of secular liberals.

'What do you want to talk about, madam?' The maulana carefully tried uttering a complete sentence without a swear word.

'Tell me, who has given you the authority to put people in misery?' Mahbanu's voice was trembling.

'This authority is given to us by our Creator. We must defend our Creator and His word from the machinations of wicked men.'

'Oh, so you are trying to defend your Creator? Isn't it supposed to be the other way round?'

'Madam, you will not understand. Please go back to your world,' the maulana was brusque.

'How do I go back to my world when you are interfering with it? I have been forced to enter your world to understand what you want from this drama.'

'It might be a drama to you, but for us it is a sacred duty.'

'Don't you know that you will be answerable to Allah for your deeds? For putting people through misery!'

'Yes, and don't you know that you will be answerable for not covering your hair?'

'Do patients die and children miss their school if I show my hair, Maulana, or does an uncovered crippled girl excite your fantasy? What is your reason? Why are you doing this? Listen to me, Maulana. You are as incapacitated as I am. I know that you also became a paraplegic as I am in an accident. But it doesn't mean that you take it out on these poor residents in the name of Allah.'

Maulana Ishaq didn't have the patience to carry on with this dialogue.

'I do not have to answer you. You go back where you came from.'

'No, I will not go back till you clear this place and let people live in peace.'

Abdul Aziz could not let his leader be insulted by a secular girl. He moved forward, shoved the nurse aside, turned the face of the wheelchair in the direction from where Mahbanu had come and pushed it as hard as he could. The thrust was so hard and abrupt that Mahbanu couldn't keep her balance and slipped off the wheelchair. The nurse rushed towards her; there was no one else to help her get back. In his rage, Abdul Aziz didn't care if the incident was being shown live across the country. Mahbanu's driver, who like thousands of other onlookers was nervously watching the large screen, couldn't resist, and after yelling out a courageous expletive at the maulana, started running towards the sit-in to bring his madam safely back. He couldn't have imagined this behaviour from the men of God towards a disabled lady. The entire country, especially the huge crowd around the venue, was shocked to see this maltreatment.

While running, he loudly urged the crowd to take the maulana and his men to task. Abdul Aziz's shove and push were being broadcasted repeatedly over all the television channels. Soon there was a commotion in the crowd as if it had woken from slumber. Some women started screaming in protest. 'Toss the priest from the pulpit,' they cried out loud. In a matter of minutes, the crowd led by women and children started moving decisively towards the sit-in to dislodge the miscreants blocking their way. The reluctant men, ambling nearby, followed.

11

Bacha Sahib

'Nothing exists outside One; the rest is all a mirage.' Bacha Sahib's soft voice pervaded through the hall. It was customary for him to deliver a talk to the participants in the mosque once the afternoon prayers were over. For the past three decades, he had made it his routine to engage with people in the afternoon. With his back resting against the wall, Bacha Sahib would lovingly welcome every person wishing to speak with him. People from faraway villages thronged to him for comfort and assistance. Fathers threw their cranky, asthmatic babies into his lap, heaving a sigh of relief as they saw them go to sleep in minutes. Men came to him writhing in pain. The consensus among people was that he was close to Allah, a position he was known to have achieved through years of curbing physical temptations and immersing himself in rigorous prayers. 'His presence is soothing,' they would say.

'At the end of the day, we go back stronger to face our troubles.'

A short, chubby man in his seventies, Bacha Sahib was a quintessential part of the village. His family had lived here for hundreds of years and was known to be genuinely pious. To achieve this badge of honour among the cynical people of the North was a great accomplishment.

The mild-mannered Bacha Sahib was too polite for his surroundings. People were shocked to find out that he had simply given his lands away to his brothers. The story was that at the time of distribution, on his father's demise, he had asked his brothers to give him whatever was left after they were satisfied with their respective portions. People belonging to landed families did not behave that way, especially in this part of the world where land formed an integral part of the Pukhtoon code of life. Although the incident had happened a long time back, village elders still shook their heads in disbelief over the abandonment of an important constituent of the Pukhtoon trait. Vendettas over land were known to continue for generations and here was a man who had given it all away without an argument.

There was nothing dramatic about Bacha Sahib in any sense of the word. Feebly assisted by his walking stick and taking short, uncertain steps, it always took him a long time to reach the mosque. Shamroz, his assistant and helper, walked behind him with his head bowed in respect. The number of people wishing to meet Bacha Sahib had swelled over the years. Generally, he was known to take questions, providing answers to their doubts, lessening their fears and rationalizing their anger. But there were times when he engaged his audience in a monologue, and when he did, people listened with reverence, registering each and every word.

Today, after he had finished clarifying a certain issue, a participant had passed a comment to the effect that there was a time when only God existed—meaning a time prior to the creation of the Universe as we know it—prompting him to smile and look at the young man affectionately before replying, 'Young man, do you believe that the situation has changed? Does anything exist outside Him? The world that you see now is just a manifestation of Him in a degree that is perceptible through our senses.'

Firmly perched in a corner, Abdul Aziz frowned at this remark and whispered to his younger brother, Abdul Rahman, 'This is blasphemy! He is equating the world with God!'

* * *

Abdul Rahman was a reluctant imam. Having been forced into this position by Saleem Khan, he was finding it extremely difficult to live up to the expectations of a prayer leader. The only reason he had accepted this position was none other than sustenance. But struggle for the temporal didn't come easy: he had to struggle against his nature. A bespectacled man with a long face and a natural brown beard, he looked too erudite for an imam. Despite being born in the house of Maulana Khushrang, he had grown up cherishing the beats of the tabla and the poetic words of the tappa. He was instinctively drawn to poetry. Over the years, he had memorized books upon books of couplets from the famous poets of the North. He ended up narrating couplets in public, knowing fully well that for an imam it wasn't acceptable. He had tried to justify his interest in the non-religious poetry, but to no avail. He tended to quote a lot from Abdul Ghani Khan, the widely popular but non-conformist poet, often raising eyebrows. The more pious villagers wondered at his worldly disposition and compared him with Noah's son, the one who had declined to board the ark and had drowned when God's punishment came. Initially they called him 'Khushrang's past sin' before settling down for the nom de guerre, 'whirling Rahman Baba'. A soft-spoken fellow, Abdul Rahman's lovable nature was so overwhelming that even the ones chastising him for his proclivity tended to like him.

Before becoming an imam, Abdul Rahman had been a regular participant at the Khan's hujra, where the local musicians performed under the patronage of Ashfaq Khan. Although he was admonished by his elder brother, he could not suppress his passion. Villagers mocked him every time they saw him and threatened to snitch on him to his father and later his brother. He would beg them to let him enjoy the evening. 'Allah will forgive me,' he would say. He often wondered why the drumbeats of a military band were not frowned upon, when both were supposed to raise passions, albeit in a different manner. Why would angels resent something he liked? An aficionado in its truest sense, as the evening would progress and the beats of the tabla would become more pronounced, he would get into a trance. He was known to have his hands clasped to his chest as he whirled, even after the music had come to an end. It was only when someone caught him and forcibly made him sit down that he would awake from his reverie. It was on an evening just like this when he was summoned by Saleem Khan to become the imam of Khan Sahib's mosque. He had resisted but Saleem Khan would have none of his excuses and he was forced to agree.

Abdul Rahman had received his religious education from the same madrasa his father Khushrang was sent to by Khan Sahib. Both seemed to have the same issue: memory. But there was a slight difference. Abdul Rahman didn't need to exert himself when it came to memorizing poetry, but had trouble learning the religious texts. If prompted, he could read out volumes upon volumes of couplets from renowned Pushto poets. What unnerved his religious teachers was the fact that he tended to quote from the poets even while making a religious argument. They became even more anxious when he excessively started quoting poetry containing wine and sensory images, arguing that these were mystical representations of Divine love. This alarming delinquency was conveyed to Khushrang, who tried to get him out of this habit by burning his poetry books, making an exception for the ones by the celebrated Sufi poet and his namesake, Abdul Rahman Baba.

Abdul Rahman had heard about books being burnt but couldn't fathom the impact when he saw it happen in his own house right in front of him. He just couldn't erase from his mind the image of the burning books. He tried to calm his mind by reminding himself that many great theologians like Ibn-e-Arabi and Imam Ghazali also had their books burnt, but then he was no theologian and he hadn't authored any books. The mental scar left by this incident did not seem to heal, and the little interest in religious education that he had forced upon himself came to a pious halt. Unable to gather anything worthwhile in his surroundings, Abdul Rahman aimlessly wandered the streets of his village, knowing he didn't have the religious aptitude to go back to his madrasa. At the same time, he also knew that he lacked the necessary skill to deal with the temporal world. Except for some half-quoted religious texts—those too requiring crutches of drunken imagery—he didn't have any other skill to live through life. What future could a madrasa dropout have in the village? He looked around but could not find anything worthwhile. People smiled at him when he asked for work. They didn't know how to deal with a half-priest.

Yes, his father also had the same occupation, but he had been anointed by Khan Sahib. The realization that a man being groomed for intercession between God and His creation didn't have the required talent to do so had shocked the village folk. And just when Abdul Rahman had lost all hope of finding a vocation, Saleem Khan asked him to take care of Khan Sahib's mosque as Khushrang had done in his life.

No one could have been happier than Abdul Aziz, who saw an opportunity in dominating the religious life of the entire village. Given his strong personality, he knew he could easily manipulate Abdul Rahman to do his bidding. His only concern was his brother's seemingly religious fickleness. Now that he had been appointed imam, he had to fully comply with the norms of the given position, which required giving up listening to music and reading poetry; watching television was out of the question. Initially, Abdul Rahman followed everything by the book. But he knew it couldn't continue for long. And then there was a musical evening arranged at the hujra. The musicians insisted on having Abdul Rahman there. Feeling pressurized, he went with the firm conviction of keeping his wits about himself, which basically meant to not start dancing. But alas, it was not to be, and the whirling Rahman Baba entertained the crowd more than they could have imagined.

Abdul Rahman was averse to conflict. He was ill at ease when people started arguing—and there were lots of disputes on petty issues. He lived in a bad-tempered society that occasionally experimented with decency. With his performance in the hujra that night, the occasional taunts became more frequent and serious in nature. 'You are an imam and should behave like one,' the villagers said to his face. Saleem Khan was told about this, but he laughed it off. 'Yes, I will tell him not to dance in front of the people. He should dance alone in a room.'

Even before Abdul Rahman was hurled mercilessly into the position of imam, he would regularly visit Bacha Sahib. He always felt relaxed when he was in Bacha Sahib's company. And now, with his reputation in tatters, he became an even more frequent visitor of Bamkhel, Bacha Sahib's village. While previously he could not afford a taxi or a tonga, now he had some means to pay for this luxury. Without feeling the need to make others aware of his presence, he would sit quietly in the mosque and listen intently to every word of Bacha Sahib.

During his initial visits, Bacha Sahib would see a young man with deep-set eyes and a scraggly brown beard sit quietly in a corner and take notes. So, one day, he asked him to come near and tell him what he was writing. He was surprised to find the detailed notes he had written, replete with dates and additional comments where required. It was then that Bacha Sahib asked him to sit closer to him and encouraged him to speak up.

'Child, why are you distracted in mind and soul?'

'Bacha Sahib, when I hear good poetry with music, it soothes me to the core. At no time do I feel wayward. There must be some melody in the Universe, isn't it, Bacha Sahib? People call me a weak believer, but I swear upon my soul not a moment takes me away from my Creator.'

Bacha Sahib realized his sincerity and started educating him intimately on spiritual techniques. Of the people who visited Bamkhel, only a handful were interested in carrying out these exercises and even among those, very few could continue. The routine was boring; it didn't lead towards anything extraordinary. The common understanding that religious meditation would reveal secrets of this world and the Universe was just not true. Unable to see anything beyond the physical realm, a frustrated Abdul Rahman did ask Bacha Sahib reluctantly if it was his limited talent or scarcity of the spiritual regimen that prevented him from achieving mystical glory. Bacha Sahib had smiled in his characteristic manner and replied, 'My dear Abdul Rahman, mysticism is no magic; it is a way of getting closer to the truth. If during that journey you come across events that could be termed as metaphysical, it is just a coincidence. Observing anything that could be termed as a miracle must not be the objective.' Abdul Rahman could only find himself staring at the chubby hands of Bacha Sahib.

Abdul Aziz was already furious with his brother. Despite his chidings, his brother had conducted himself in a manner unbecoming of his position. On top of that, his visits to Bacha Sahib had become more frequent. Every trip meant a chance for someone else to lead prayers in his absence. Consistency was extremely important for an imam. Abdul Aziz was apprehensive that if his brother lost this mosque to someone else, his own position would weaken, and he didn't want to let go of the privileges it offered. So, one day, he decided to make a joint visit to Bamkhel with his brother to see what it was all about.

* * *

'So, you tell me that Bacha Sahib is a great mystic. He electrifies you when he hugs you. Let us see if he can read my mind from here. When we meet him, we should be served boiled eggs and halwa made from nuts. I will not consider him a mystic if we are not served the two things I have mentioned.' As Abdul Aziz conveyed his understanding of mysticism, Abdul Rahman looked up at him in a questioning manner. 'He is a mystic, not a magician. Only Allah is aware of what goes on in our hearts.'

'What about the tall claims I hear from you about people being healed and thieves being caught after being identified by him? He should be able to read my mind as well.'

'Brother, I suggest you do not meet him if you are going with this objective,' Abdul Rahman said dejectedly. 'Please do not go to test his credentials. You should go with the aim of gaining something.'

'And what does he have to offer, my little brother? Spirituality? There is nothing in the Sharia defining spirituality. We need to confirm if he is a firm follower of the Sharia or not. You know there are a lot of charlatans masquerading as men of God just to make money.'

'No, he doesn't take any money,' Abdul Rahman replied firmly.

'Well, let us meet him and find out.'

'And, by the way, my sources tell me that those he asks to lead the prayers consider it a matter of great privilege.'

'Yes,' Abdul Rahman replied. 'There is no imam in his mosque. Due to arthritis, he cannot stand upright for long to lead the prayers and so he asks someone he believes is the right person to lead. It is no doubt a privilege to lead the prayers in his mosque.'

'If he can't heal his own arthritis, what good can he do to others?'

'He is a spiritual guide only and does not claim to be anything else.' Abdul Rahman was visibly upset with his brother, whose scepticism was irritating him.

'Abdul Rahman, let us go, and I'll see for myself. And if he is spiritually enlightened, he would know who has the ability and the training to lead prayers.'

'I have seen people who come regularly never being asked to lead, while there are others who are asked to lead on their first visit.'

'Has he ever asked you to lead?' Abdul Aziz asked him derisively.

'No, he hasn't, and I do not need to be asked. But he gives me lot of attention and time.'

* * *

Bacha Sahib was almost alone in the mosque when the brothers arrived. The two men sitting with him earlier were on their way out. Looking at the brothers no one could imagine they were related by blood: one too dusky and the other as fair as a Pukhtoon is expected to be. Even their features didn't have anything in common; Khushrang's genes were meant for Abdul Aziz alone. As they sat down and settled themselves on the floor in front of Bacha Sahib, Abdul Rahman introduced his brother. Abdul Aziz stared rudely at this short man, whose chubby appearance conveyed to him a lack of hard work. His round face exuded serenity in a pensive sense. The only thing he could not help admiring was the colour of henna Bacha Sahib had used to dye his beard. He found the deep maroon to be much more acceptable compared to the ugly reddish tinge he generally saw. After the initial pleasantries, Bacha Sahib addressed Abdul Aziz, 'It is always better to come with an open mind instead of being sceptical.' Not expecting a comment of the sort and without having said anything, Abdul Aziz was visibly distraught. He could do nothing but squirm. However, Bacha Sahib didn't pursue his comment further and let him off by mentioning the cold weather. After a while, the discussion turned to spirituality.

'No, you do not require spirituality to practise religion,' was Bacha Sahib's reply to Abdul Aziz's query. 'You could still be a good Muslim without practising it. Pursuit of mysticism is only for the willing.'

The discussion on mysticism and spirituality carried on for a while. Visitors had started entering the mosque and sat quietly listening to the exchange. After some time, Bacha Sahib's attendant, Shamroz, came to ask the two gentlemen to accompany them for tea in the side room. Originally built for the imam, the room was used for serving snacks to those who came from outside the village. Bacha Sahib took it upon himself to serve food and tea to all the outside guests.

A heavily patterned cloth covered the plates and the dishes as usual. As Shamroz removed the cloth, the brothers were surprised to find boiled eggs and halwa made from nuts. They kept quiet during tea, with Abdul Aziz contemplating how to interpret this chance occurrence of getting what he had asked for and Abdul Rahman feeling ecstatic over the mystical strength of Bacha Sahib. After having finished, they left the room and sat in a corner of the mosque hall, where a large number of people had gathered and were listening intently to Bacha Sahib.

After having listened for a while, Abdul Aziz whispered his blasphemy remark to Abdul Rahman, who did not seem to listen. Bacha Sahib went ahead with his talk, finally quoting *Ibn-e-Arabi*,

> *I follow the religion of love whichever way its camels take;*
> *For this is my religion and my faith.*

Abdul Aziz frowned and looked around but couldn't find any supporters. In the Sharia, there was no concept of religion of love. There was one religion and it was Islam. He strongly believed that Bacha Sahib was committing *bidaa* (innovation) by mentioning things that didn't exist in religion.

As he finished the quote, Bacha Sahib looked around for questions. And then came the oft-repeated question that has intrigued every follower of religion since the beginning of Divine religion itself. A young participant asked, Bacha Sahib, 'If we believe all actions to be from Allah, then why are we held responsible for them?'

Bacha Sahib's face lit up as he replied. 'It is man's nature that is predestined, not his actions. This matter must be cleared once and for all to everyone. Your form is predetermined and so are your movements. What you carry out from those predestined movements is your own doing; don't blame Him for your intentions and actions. And mind you, by disobeying him you are still carrying out His creative command but breaking only His religious command.'

Bacha Sahib had barely finished when a dishevelled tramp entered the mosque. Clearly demented, the poor man was desperately trying to wrap himself with the blanket he was carrying. He just couldn't get it right; as he tried to cover his shoulders, the blanket would always slip to his waist. His unkempt hair and beard were thick with dust. But it was the look on his face that clearly showed his disconnection with the world around him. As he entered the hall, his loud, unintelligible whining alerted the people. They all turned around, but surprisingly no one got up to stop him. As soon as the tramp set his eyes on Bacha Sahib, his expression transformed from misery to a madman's wide grin. To Abdul Aziz's surprise, he went straight to Bacha Sahib, prostrated in front of him, caught his feet and in doing so let out a loud whimper. Bacha Sahib put both his hands on his back and started caressing him, 'My friend Junaid is here. I am so glad to see you Junaid. You came after so many days.' All Junaid managed to utter was a repetitive 'Bacha Sahib' in the manner of a child, while Bacha Sahib caressed his back lovingly with both his hands. The effusion from Junaid's nose and the tears from his eyes, as he sobbed loudly, made his beard sticky.

'Junaid, my child, you have suffered a lot. May Allah have mercy on you!' And then, addressing the congregation, he said, 'This child, Junaid, has found nothing in existence but Allah himself.' He then turned towards the person in attendance on him, 'Shamroz, take Junaid Khan to the guest room; wash him, give him new clothes and feed him well. Make sure he is properly covered; he already seems to be suffering from exposure to cold.'

By this time, Abdul Aziz could not contain his disappointment any longer and could not help asking, 'But he is a blasphemer. Why should he be treated with kindness? He should be hanged to death.'

To address Bacha Sahib in that manner and to question his action was impudent. There was visible unease among the participants.

'Abdul Aziz, we are built in God's image, right? How can the image become so distorted so as to condemn people to death? Why are we congregated here in this mosque? We are here to bring out the Divine in ourselves and not to let it die. To let that Divine die is murder; that is real blasphemy! You are a student of Sharia, so tell me. What is the criterion for a religious thought to be correct or incorrect?' Bacha Sahib looked up at Abdul Aziz inquiringly.

Bacha Sahib could see Abdul Aziz frantically searching his memory chips for an answer. The teaching he had received at the madrasa had left him with no room for lateral thinking. He lacked perspective on almost everything except what he had been taught. As his eyes wandered frantically looking for an answer,

Bacha Sahib intervened, 'Let me tell you. Any thought that strives to preserve life is in accordance with Sharia; anything against is incorrect.'

'But are we not to condemn a blasphemer?'

'And who has given you the authority to condemn anyone?' Bacha Sahib's firm tone made Abdul Aziz tense as he felt everyone staring at him.

Unwilling to back off so easily, he tried to change the subject and asked if an imam was allowed to indulge in music and poetry.

'Abdul Aziz, do you ask this unrelated question for someone in particular or for the guidance of the public at large?'

Abdul Rahman ground his teeth, wanting his brother to stop arguing with Bacha Sahib.

'No, I ask for the sake of the general public.' Abdul Aziz tried to make it sound simple.

'You never create the love of Allah in the hearts of people by reading to them the covenants of Sharia.'

No one had ever seen Bacha Sahib speak pointedly to anyone in that firm a tone. The congregation was not impressed with Abdul Aziz's impudence; there were murmurs of disagreement against him.

Given the mood of the congregation, Abdul Aziz thought it best to back off. Bacha Sahib then asked Abdul Rahman to sit closer to him and asked him about his exercise routine. He then pointed at a spot in the middle of the chest, 'This spot here is the place of love for your Creator. For the next forty days you need to concentrate here with the words I had taught you the last time you were here.'

Bacha Sahib then leaned back and called out, 'Gentlemen, it is time for Muraqaba, concentration, now.' A lull descended as everyone closed their eyes and bowed their heads. Tempted to see what was happening around him, Abdul Aziz opened one eye and surveyed the room. Everyone seemed to have descended into a state of deep sleep, albeit without snoring. No one coughed or cleared their throats; there wasn't even a rustle of clothes. He looked sideways at Abdul Rahman, but it was no use. Nobody seemed to be aware of the other. He tried stifling his yawn but couldn't help it. It was only when the muezzin called for the evening prayers that Bacha Sahib's loud 'Alhumdulillah' woke everyone up.

The time had arrived for the chosen one to lead the prayers. As Bacha Sahib surveyed the congregation, his eyes rested on Abdul Rahman. He smiled at him and announced, 'Today Abdul Rahman will lead the evening prayers.'

Acknowledgements

First of all, I would like to acknowledge my friend, Dr Osama Siddique, a novelist himself, who guided me in placing this book in the right hands.

I am greatly indebted to the professionalism of Elizabeth Kuruvilla, the editor, Saloni Mital, the copy editor, and Rinjini Mitra for the marketing effort. Working with these professionals was such a pleasure.